More Advance Praise for Relative Strangers

"A talented, versatile writer, Margaret Hermes has given us a highly original collection with many gems. 'Growing Season,' 'The Bee Queen,' and 'For the Home Team' are particularly delightful."

—DAVID CARKEET, author of *Double Negative* and *The Full Catastrophe*

"Margaret Hermes writes of the sexuality of educated women with a candor and precision unseen since Kate Chopin."

—PETER LEACH, author of *Gone By Sundown* and *Tales of Resistance*

"What I love best about the stories of Margaret Hermes is their atmosphere of an enduring eroticism, of passions wreathed in the incense of autumnal woodsmoke as the days shorten and darken and seasons change and love anticipates its final harvest. *Relative Strangers* is a wise and confident collection by an exquisitely talented writer."

—BOB SHACOCHIS, National Book Award-winning author of *Easy in the Islands* and *Swimming in the Volcano*

"With tongue firmly in cheek, Margaret Hermes writes about missed connections between lovers, between grandparents and parents and children and friends. More than that, she writes with humor and wisdom about women who confuse sex for love and love for sex and cannot decide which one they prefer."

—MARY TROY, author of *Beauties* and *The Albi Café*

"Lively and humorous, *Relative Strangers* gives a reader something to enjoy and admire on every page."

—JANE O. WAYNE, Devins Award and the Society of Midland Authors Poetry Award-winning author of *The Other Place You Live* and *Looking Both Ways*

For Amy,

Relative Strangers

SHORT STORIES by MARGARET HERMES

with love,

Margaret Hermes

Carolina Wren Press

© 2012 Margaret Hermes

Editor: Andrea Selch
Copyeditor: Kay Robin Alexander
Design: Lesley Landis Designs
Author Photograph and
  Cover Image by Lucy Hg © 2011

The mission of Carolina Wren Press is to seek out, nurture, and promote literary work by new and underrepresented writers, including women and writers of color.

This publication was made possible by Michael Bakwin's generous establishment of the Doris Bakwin Award for Writing by a Woman, and the continued support of Carolina Wren Press by the extended Bakwin family. We gratefully acknowledge the ongoing support of general operations by the Durham Arts Council's United Arts Fund.

Library of Congress Cataloging-in-Publication Data

Hermes, Margaret.
Relative strangers : short stories / Margaret Hermes.
p. cm.
ISBN 978-0-932112-62-0 (alk. paper)
I. Title.

PS3558.E686R45 2012
813'.54--dc23

ACKNOWLEDGMENTS

Stories here originally appeared, sometimes in slightly different versions, in the following magazines and anthologies, to whose editors grateful acknowledgment is made: "The Bee Queen" first appeared in *Sou'wester*; "Growing Season" in *Wisconsin Review*; "Transubstantiation" in *The Laurel Review* and subsequently in the anthology *20 Over 40*, published by the University Press of Mississippi. "Relative Strangers" also debuted in *The Laurel Review*; "Over Easy" in *The Madison Review*; "Meet Me" in *Art Times*; "Without Windows" in *Red Cedar Review*; "The River's Daughter" in *Talking River Review*; "Second Lover" in *Under the Arch*, an anthology from Antares Press; "Foreign Exchange" in *River Styx*; "Parings" in *Phoebe*; "Dance of the Hours" in *The Literary Review*; and "For the Home Team" in *The Secret Alameda*. "Sorting," which won first prize in The Write Stuff short fiction contest, appeared in *St. Louis Weekly*.

My profound thanks to my writer – and reader! – friends whose insights and encouragement have been invaluable. I remain happily indebted to my first readers, my partner David Garin and my astute and sensitive daughters Sarah Hermes Griesbach and Lucy Hermes Griesbach (media artist Lucy Hg). I wish to salute Carolina Wren Press for its tradition of publishing handsomely-produced books, often by writers historically neglected by mainstream publishers. My gratitude also to the family of the late Doris Bakwin, whose endowment of the award given in her name brings recognition to women writers and support to the mission of a small, dedicated, nonprofit press.

for David

} CONTENTS {

} THE BEE QUEEN {

When Bette died at age sixty-four the townspeople erected a stone to her, a companion piece to that of her deceased husband Leon. Hewn in pink marble were the words

Bette Louise Trimble
1902–1966
Valedictorian 1919
Felled by Wasps

Bette would have been both gratified and annoyed by the inscription. Her last years, which saw the burying of her own parents, put her to wondering if, when the time came, there would be anybody around to spell her name properly. When the time came she was sure she'd be weary enough of a lifetime of saying no, not Betty, never Elizabeth, just B-e-t-t-e.

Even when Dr. Alfele surprised her by including her name right after his graduate student's on his paper titled *The Generational Migration of Carpenter Bees*, it wasn't her name after all. The list read: Jorge L. Alfele, Theodore Roosevelt Bynum, Elizabeth Trimble. Despite fourteen years of correspondence with the professor, she supposed that he supposed her real name must be something more. Dr. Alfele had meant only kindness, of course, and she recollected how her own father had written B-e-t-t-y on the 1920 census form.

For a while, when she was fifteen, she had been "Bettelou" at school.

The name had looked French to her and under its influence she learned to wear a beret – grey flannel – and exhale cigarette smoke through her nostrils. As no other girls at the high school smoked, it was easy to acquire a reputation for being fast – she hardly had to exert herself.

Two blocks from school she would pull a small wad of newspaper from the pocket of her navy wool jacket and unwrap a stub of charred cork. She would light a match against the postal box and sear the tired piece of cork. With the aid of a two-by-three-inch purse mirror which was losing its silvering, she'd dab at the soot with her index finger and daub worldly, French hollows beneath her eyes. As she examined her reflection, Bette would wonder if Lady With was alive and wearing store-bought cosmetics. But Lady With had been so beautiful Bette couldn't imagine any human artistry improving her appearance.

All experimentation was brought to a halt when the twins entered high school. It would have been lunacy to continue and so she became just Bette again. The boys would have reported her to their parents and her mother would have waited for her outside the kitchen until Bette had finished her bath, until all her pores were open and her skin was at its most tender, to mutely (righteous beyond words) take a switch to her. No, when the twins arrived at high school, the dark circles disappeared from Bette's eyes and the beret was anchored with an imitation pearl hatpin to keep it from slouching to its former rakish angle.

Her teachers noticed the change and were much easier on Bette. They gave her more attention once they thought they had reformed her, so she did well enough at school to earn rare praise at home. "Maybe you'll make something of yourself," her mother said with some surprise, putting forth the notion for the first time when Bette awkwardly set her prize-winning essay *Our Founding Fathers* on the kitchen table. "Go on," Bette scoffed, blushing at the unprecedented flattery, but soon after she stopped telling Augustus Blue, Class of 1917, that she needed more time to decide "if maybe I will and maybe I won't." Bette told him she'd rather die instead and she made a valedictorian out of herself, the top in her class of twenty-six in Tallapoosa in 1919.

Tallapoosa was situated in that part of Missouri called the Bootheel. Bette's father liked to say that the Bootheel was cobbled just for stepping on the necks of the sons of bitches who lived there, but Bette's mother would say "Language!" just as quick and then "What do you know about it?" with just as much satisfaction.

Bette guessed that her father was casting aspersions on her mother's family tree (her father's people came from Virginia and were regarded by him as "coastal" even though he himself had seen the Atlantic only once) but very little passed for conversation in their house so she never did know for certain which sons of bitches her daddy referred to. She did know for certain that a little flare-up about these vague relations every now and then was the most you could hope for from him.

After graduation Bette was scheming to go to the Normal School and get her certification but her father injured his back carrying a wringer washer down the basement steps and could no longer climb a ladder to do roofing work and gutter repairs. The twins had two more years of high school, so Bette started working nine to five at Trimble's selling "Shoes for the Discriminating Foot." Bette did well at the shoe store. Many customers asked to be fitted by her over Leon Trimble himself. Trimble would sell a shoe to a customer but Bette would sell the shoe to a foot. "Now, how does that *feel?*" she'd say with a sober, considering look. "I think we'd better put that foot into a shoe that understands arch support." While her emphasis was on comfort, Bette never disregarded style. She told Mr. Trimble he'd better update his old-lady shoes. "These look like they've already got bunions built into them."

For years Bette continued on at *Trimble's*, living at her parents', dating the occasional traveling shoe salesman. The local boys respected her, even let her advise them on their footwear, but not one had the courage to court this plainspoken female who was publicly certified as smarter. So Bette sold shoes to her former beaux. She fitted them with black lace-ups for their weddings, with cordovan wingtips for their jobs, and with spiked brogues for the golf course.

And she sold shoes to their wives. When Lily Beecher née Gentry came looking for pumps for the Kiwanis dance, Bette said, "If this were my store, there would be no three- or four-inch womanslayers in stock, but it's your foot, Lily Gentry," implying that it wasn't her foot at all, that it was on loan, like a library book, and she had better take good care of it. "Now, I personally think your ankle would be shown to its best advantage in one of these sassy, strappy things here." Bette unwrapped a low-heeled sandal from its tissue and held it up reverentially. "But maybe you want an excuse for sitting out all those dances? Maybe Walter Beecher will be satisfied dancing with all those women who've been buying evening slippers with a danceable heel. I don't know."

The shop did well right through the Depression. Being the only shoe store serving five townships helped, but some folks thought the reason wasn't just that *Trimble's* carried dependable shoes or that Bette was a good saleswoman, but that she knew how to slip in a foot massage when a customer got peevish. People felt good coming out of *Trimble's* and they felt good wearing shoes from *Trimble's*. Very occasionally, after she pulled down the dark green window shade with "Shoes for the Discriminating Foot" on it and the shop was closed for the day, Bette would instruct Mr. Trimble to sit and she would slip off his fringe-tongued oxford in brown and white and give him a foot massage. It was during one of these that Mr. Trimble asked Bette to marry him and she said yes.

Then he got up from the leather customer's chair he'd been sitting in and pulled her up from the little wooden stool she was perched on and gently guided her onto the leather chair. He sat down on the stool facing her and lifted her right foot and slipped off her camel-colored pump with its sensible but refined stacked wooden heel and stroked and kneaded the sole of her instep. Then he did the same for the other foot.

Most people in Tallapoosa were surprised by the wedding. There had been some speculation that Leon Trimble was a fairy who didn't bother anybody, so Leon's mother was pleased by the marriage. Bette's mother was not. It was impossible to tell what Bette's father thought. He was one of Bette's failures: he always looked like his shoes pinched.

Bette and Leon – she called him Mr. Trimble at the store; she said she would have called him Leon if the store had been called *Leon's* but now there was no turning back – didn't have any children. Some people speculated that wasn't all they didn't have, but the pair seemed content to share the business, and the crossword puzzle they solved together each evening, and their week in Florida each February, and their week in Michigan each August.

Bette was still a reader and by now she had read the extended works of all the authors who had piqued her interest back in high school. She could have discussed Nathaniel Hawthorne's *Marble Faun* if anybody else in Tallapoosa had read it. She also read some history and travel and plenty of how-to books. The only type of reading she absolutely scorned was autobiography. "I like my fiction to be called fiction," she said to her father, who had no idea what she was talking about. "Life is stranger than fiction," Bette's mother said, "and that's a fact." Bette thought of that and of Lady With the day she was stung.

} {

Bette was on the annual Second Presbyterian Church picnic with Leon and his mother (her parents were across town at the Methodist affair) when she slipped off her shoes – not because her feet hurt but because she liked the feel of grass between her toes. She had come bare-legged to the picnic in anticipation. When she set out across the grass to retrieve Brian Lovejoy's kite, which had plunged suspiciously and landed in the azaleas near where the girls were sunning themselves and collecting blooms for their flower presses, she stepped on something sharp amid the clover. Startled, her mouth circled around an "Oh!" She looked at her foot. "Bumblebee," she said before she collapsed. Fortunately, Ora Smith had also come to investigate Brian's kite. He ran for Dr. Lawless who was enjoying the elder Mrs. Trimble's cornflake-crumbed fried chicken in the shade of a sweetgum tree. The doctor was relieved to find Bette sitting upright, holding tight to young Brian Lovejoy's shoulder. "Well?" he said. Being the only doctor in town, he hadn't needed to develop a bedside manner.

"Well, that sting just took me by surprise. Took my breath away," Bette said.

"Shallow breathing," Dr. Lawless nodded as he placed two fingers across the inside of Bette's wrist. "Rapid pulse," he nodded again. "Antihistamines," he said as he pulled a physician's sample packet of small yellow tablets from his black bag. "For the localized reaction. Prescription," he said as he wrote on a small white pad, "for the next time."

"I don't expect there will be a next time," Bette considered. "Odds are against it."

"As your physician, Bette, I am ordering you to get this prescription filled and keep it on hand."

Ora Smith was impressed. "What's it for, Doc?"

"A shot of adrenalin in case her body plumb shuts down the next time. Mrs. Trimble is allergic. You've never been stung by a bee before?" he turned back to Bette.

"No, never. I thought somehow I couldn't get stung."

"Well, let's hope you go another forty years without a sting."

"I don't mind saying I'm just as glad it didn't happen any sooner." Some people, Bette knew, who were stung early in life, never got over the experience. As though it were yesterday, she could see eight-year-old Lady With lying like a treasured porcelain doll, rigid and exquisite.

} {

Bette's experience of being stung didn't make her fearful, though the injection prescribed by Dr. Lawless in the event of another sting did make her uneasy. "I'm not afraid of shots," she said to Bob Bracey, the pharmacist at the Rexall Drugs two doors down from Trimble's, "I'm just leery of this one. Epinephrine," Bette read off the package.

"Fake adrenalin," Bob Bracey explained. "I want you to keep this in the fridge. This stuff can go bad on you."

Even if it didn't go bad, it could be pretty bad, Bette read. The injection itself could cause "cerebral hemorrhage due to a sharp rise in blood pressure," according to the enclosed pamphlet. The "transient and minor" side effects included palpitation, respiratory difficulty, pallor, dizziness, weakness, tremor, headache, throbbing, restlessness, tenseness, anxiety, fear, and ventricular arrhythmias. Bette wondered how you could tell if the injection was working as those were pretty much the symptoms Dr. Lawless had said to watch out for if she were stung.

"Now, remember," said Bob, Class of 1926, "it is paramount" – "paramount" was a word he'd picked up at pharmacy school and he dispensed it with every prescription – "absolutely paramount that you carry your injector kit with you at all times. Your life could depend on it."

Bette chuckled all the way back to the store. Keeping the injector both refrigerated and with her at all times conjured up some happy visions of heading for work with a small Frigidaire strapped to her back or borrowing the Good Humor truck whenever she and Leon wanted to drive into the Ozarks.

She put her injector kit at the back of the top shelf of her refrigerator and pretty well forgot about it except when she cleaned the shelves and ritualistically returned the epinephrine and the unopened jar of her mother's calf's foot jelly to that top left-hand corner.

For more than three decades she had batted away all stray thoughts of stinging creatures, her uneasiness stifling her natural curiosity. One day, six months after the Second Presbyterian annual picnic, while standing in front of the shelf of golden honey at the IGA, Bette finally made up her mind to read all she could about native wasps and bees.

She studied the question of stinging insects with the thoroughness of a valedictorian. She learned about the differences between solitary and social species, about species that burrow into the ground and the mud daubers and paper wasps that build up their nests like masons, and about the honey producers with their astonishing, complicated hives.

Bette became something of an expert and, as happens with any expertise, she found it hard not to share morsels of her knowledge. She told Leon things like: The sand wasp is often misunderstood; it's not attacking the person it keeps buzzing around but just trying to catch the flies that are attracted to that person. Leon would listen with his eyebrows raised, then nod his head and smile. Sometimes he would pat her cheek.

"Did you know that honeybees are the state insect of Missouri?" she said to her parents one Thanksgiving when they were gathered at one of the twins' houses for dinner.

"That so?" her father said, puzzled. He'd had a stroke the year before and since then his sentences had grown even shorter.

"Next thing they'll be electing a state weed and a state disease," her mother said.

"That's Missour-uh for you," her father aimed at her mother, showing that the stroke had left some part of him unimpaired after all.

Bette tried to remember to speak of her interest in stinging insects only to Leon. She found out that the tiger-striped bugs she had grown up calling sweat bees were really a kind of yellowjacket and that their nests could contain as many as 5,000 aggressive wasps. Real sweat bees were green and peace-loving. She was tempted to correct her mother the next time Mrs. Melroy shooed a black and yellow "sweat bee," but she knew her mother would not have been grateful for the instruction.

}{

Leon died in 1948 of a heart attack while standing on a ladder reaching for a pair of terra sienna brogues with tasseled laces. Bette wasn't at the store. Leon himself had insisted she come in late that morning, after she stopped by the library to look over the booklet the librarian had set aside for her that had just arrived from the state Conservation Department.

Bette was reading about velvet ants, really not ants at all but furry wasps with extraordinarily long stingers and extraordinarily painful stings, "hence the popular name 'cow killer,'" when the librarian tapped her on the shoulder and whispered, though there was no one else to hear, that there was some trouble at the store. Leaving her cardigan sweater to warm the arms of her chair and her pocketbook tucked beneath the table, she said to herself maybe the store had been descended upon by a swarm of customers, prompting an SOS from Leon, but the honeyed librarian's voice buzzed in her ears like an alarm.

Bette missed Leon from that first day. She missed sharing her meals, and the business, and the crossword puzzle, and the article in the National Geographic on the giant bees of the Philippines. She kept on at the store. It never occurred to her to do anything else. "I'm grateful that Mr. Trimble lived to see the world at peace," Bette told their customers and then she wondered, as she did at all such times, if Lady With had grown up and seen it come to pass as well.

}{

Informed by decades of novel reading, it was Bette's opinion that everyone had a "pivotal experience" in their early years and she counted Lady With as hers. (Being so particular about the spelling of her own name, she would have enjoyed the irony in discovering that she had, since age six, been reverently misspelling Lady Wyth.) When Bette was six years old she had taken the train with her mother to Roanoke, Virginia, to wait for her father's mother to die. Her father said he would just be in the way and her mother said it was her Christian duty and Bette never knew why she, rather than the twins or none of them at all, was chosen to accompany her mother on this journey.

The old woman took nearly two weeks to accomplish the deed so Bette was pretty much on her own while her mother kept vigil. Bette took up with a neighbor child, an eight-year-old girl with inky blue-black hair that peaked dramatically on her opalescent forehead. Her portentous (to Bette's ears) name and her striking appearance sent shivers of pleasure through Bette. Years later, reading *Gone With The Wind*, Bette had been suddenly, forcibly struck by her vision of a grown Lady With in the role of Scarlett. Nothing could entice Bette to see the movie with Vivien Leigh in the lead when it played in Tallapoosa.

Lady With was neither unaware nor unappreciative of Bette's adoration and so she strove to both arouse and reward the adorer. She wore starched ribbons in her heavy, long hair. She taught Bette clapping games. She held her breath for as long as it took Bette to recite the whole of "Early In The Morning In The Middle Of The Night Two Dead Boys Got Up To Fight." She showed Bette her arrowhead and her coin collection from Italy and Canada. She jumped across the creek at its deepest spot. She ran up alone onto the porch of the abandoned green shingle house with no windows and knocked on the door twice.

The day her grandmother died, Bette was off with Lady With down by the creek. Lady With had climbed the wild cherry tree that hung over the creek while wearing a white dress with red stripes and a red handkerchief triangle-stitched into the breast pocket. She was afraid of tearing her dress and was paying more attention to it than to where she was going. That's probably why she didn't see the wasp nest.

Bette had never before heard, had never imagined such screams, not even when one of the twins got scalded with potato water and the potato peels stuck, burnt into his skin like branding irons. Lady With tumbled from the tree and hurtled herself home, the black bugs adhering to her like beads of tar. Bette ran alongside her, crying but unstung. At Lady With's door her mother gathered her collapsed form into the darkness without a word or look to Bette, who stood on the porch ashamed that her own chest and arms and legs were bare of these pinned-on badges of honor.

Bette ran on to the sagging front porch of her grandmother's house but was stopped at the door by a tall, gaunt woman she had never seen before. Bette stared at the buttons of her flowered dress, dark red circles, the color of cough syrup, with a bright jewel winking in each center. "Who are you, child?" The buttons danced.

"Bette Louise Melroy."

"Why, of course you are." The woman lowered herself so that she almost perched on the heels of her black-laced shoes. "You must have already heard about your poor grandma." She pulled a white handkerchief with blue crocheted edging from inside the cuff of her dress sleeve and wiped at Bette's cheeks.

"The wasps were eating Lady With," Bette said.

The woman frowned and stood up. The line of shimmering buttons came back into view. "That's too bad," she said.

"Will she die?" Bette asked.

Bette's mother appeared in the doorway, her sleeves rolled up, slipping the collar of a bib apron over her head. "Your grandmother has already passed," she said. "She made a fine death. I believe she saw Jesus just there at the end." Then she disappeared into the house.

"Your mam is busy now. We're getting your grandmother ready," the tall woman said. "You'd best go on playing with Lady Wyth."

Bette sat down on the sloping cellar door by the side of her grandmother's house where no one could see her and wonder why she wasn't someplace else.

After the burial, when the grownups came back to her grandmother's house for plates of ham and biscuits with eleven different kinds of jelly, Bette stole down the road to Lady With's small, stone house. She crept quietly up the porch stairs, stopping at the window to the left of the front door. The dining room was more than empty; it was still, as though the family had gone away on holiday.

The other front window framed the sitting room. Bette saw Lady With's mother and father sitting stiffly on the only straightback chairs in the room, not looking at each other. Lady With was laid out on the sofa. Bette thought she looked like an angel, her translucent skin as otherworldly as any halo.

On the train back to Tallapoosa Bette said, "I wonder if Lady With saw Jesus at her end."

Her mother said, "What kind of fool talk is that?"

"When Lady With died she could have maybe seen Jesus too, or do you have to be old?"

"Well, Bette Louise, I guess I shouldn't be surprised that this trip didn't add anything to your small store of common sense. What makes you think that Lady With died?"

"I saw her. Through the window."

"What you saw is something called paralysis. What was in your ears at your grandma's supper? It's an amazement to me you didn't hear the talk: Lady With is frozen and can't move."

Bette imagined the stingers injecting ice into the veins of Lady With.

} {

On the eve of her wedding, Bette asked her mother if she had ever learned what had finally become of Lady With. "Did she ever thaw out?" she said. At that moment, everything seemed sad and funny to Bette.

"Now, how would I know?" her mother shook her head. "Your grandma was the last of your father's people in Roanoke. I didn't even have acquaintance with the neighbor ladies who helped me lay her out."

Bette decided right there and then she would write to the family. "Do you remember Lady With's last name?"

"A person can't remember what she never knew. Lady With was your friend, not mine."

Occasionally, between customers or over a particularly puzzling crossword, Bette would wonder if Lady With was still alive. She wondered if she had stayed beautiful, if she had become valedictorian. She wondered if she had married, if she had children. Once when she was fitting a customer with fallen arches, Bette was struck by the idea that if Lady With were paralyzed still, she might never in all those intervening years have ever worn a pair of shoes. A startled "My!" burst from her lips and when the customer asked "What is it?" Bette said she thought she might have left the iron plugged in and she'd better run home to check. But instead of going home she stopped at the lending library. Bette took a collection of monographs down from the shelf. It was in that collection that she first came across the work of Dr. Alfele.

She opened the volume to the page of biographical notes and copied down both his full name and his university address. Her resolve to write to a professor seemed to her no more bold than her resolve to write to such a foreign-sounding name.

Bette continued her study of the order Hymenoptera (from the Greek words hymen, which means "membrane," and pteron, which means "wing," so "membrane-winged") and the suborder Aculeata (from the Latin word aculeus, which means "sting"), sharing with Dr. Alfele her research on wasps and bees as pollinators and as the predators of cicadas, spiders, flies, and caterpillars.

"Mosquitoes are pests," she once said to Lily Beecher. "But a wasp is the Thomas à Becket of the insect world."

Lily said to her husband that Bette really could have made something of herself – a certified public accountant or the high school principal – if she'd just had some advantages.

Leon was no longer around to gently remind folks by saluting her as his Bee Queen that Bette *had* made something of herself. Whenever he had spoken of her so, Bette had blushed publicly and thought privately of Lady With, her Lady in waiting.

} {

One rainy afternoon in early November, Bette posted the large SALE sign in the store window, a rare occurrence at *Trimble's*. It had never been Bette's strategy to carry "a line" of shoes. "Different tastes, different feet, different choices," she'd said to more than one perplexed salesman over the years. "We're here to accommodate the feet," she chastised, "not make the feet accommodate the merchandise." And more often than you'd think, a pair of shoes that had sat on the shelf for a dozen years would be the answer to someone's podiatric prayers. But occasionally *Trimble's* would hold a sale so Bette could display the shoes that no one would ever imagine were there for the asking. There was a pair of sky-blue suede men's oxfords, 9½ D, just waiting for a young man who didn't need to ride the crest of a fashion wave. And Bette kept dusted the box containing pongee ankle-strapped platforms flecked with shimmering gold threads, "sturdy but flirty" she thought them. And there were others: "Anomalies," she would explain matter-of-factly, pointing to the boxes that occupied the top shelf of the twelve-foot storage wall. Bette was handing down boxes to Ora Smith's boy Everett who was working in the store for an hour every day after school. She was poised at the very top of the ladder, held steady on its rollers by hooks that clamped onto the shelves. Everett wondered how long it would be before Mrs. Trimble allowed him to retrieve stock with the ladder.

"Set those on the counter, Everett. There are three more boxes I've decided on. I think ten pair is a respectable number for a sale display, don't you?" But she didn't listen for his answer because she was busy tugging at a dark corner of the shelf. "Some kind of toy or something stuck in here," she called down. "Can you imagine? Looks like a sweet potato."

"A what?" Everett called back. He thought if she were imagining toy sweet potatoes he might need someone to help him get her down.

"You know, an ocarina."

Everett didn't know.

"A sort of flute," she said, prying with her fingers. "You blow into it. It has fingering holes." Just as she said this Bette realized an ocarina could not be wedged into this remote corner of a shoe store. She knew then what she had found, even before the beautiful metallic-blue wasps flew out from the neat, vertical row of holes. Even at the pinnacle of her predicament, Bette savored the irony of the Bee Queen's failure to recognize her own specialty out of context.

The slender, thread-waisted mud daubers dived at her in panic and circled before she tumbled from the ladder.

An autopsy showed she hadn't been stung. Bette could have saved Doc Lawless the time as she had known that mud daubers are unlikely to sting, even when aroused. The cause of death was a cerebral hemorrhage that resulted from striking her head on the standing brass ashtray in the course of her fall. Lily Beecher said it was very romantic and fitting that Bette should die years later just two feet away from where Leon Trimble had come to rest.

Bette would have been pleased that the town saw fit to erect a stone to her memory and gratified that her name was spelled right after all, but she would have been mad as a hornet at their putting the blame on the wasps.

} GROWING SEASON {

I was sent to the farm for my fifteenth summer because it was thought my presence might further disturb my mother. She was sick after losing the baby so near the end of term.

My mother seemed to have the habit of losing babies – girl babies at any rate. When I was younger I wondered if her hanging on to me hadn't been a mistake, or if afterwards she'd lost the others because she regretted her tenacity in my case. Just the sight of me seemed to upset her in those precarious times. Instead of intensifying our connection, each successive miscarriage somehow alienated her further from me. Years later my Aunt Mimi explained that my mother had longed unremittingly for a daughter, like a mermaid might long for the sea.

My father, who had some insight into municipal bonds and city management, only saw me through my mother's eyes. The military school where I boarded stopped after tenth grade, so where my parents would be sending me in the fall was the subject they fell upon every time I left the room.

I was not unhappy to be leaving the school where I had spent the last four years and three miscarriages. I had made no real friends among my classmates. My roommate, the only other Jew, had walled himself within a fortress of books at a school that valued discipline more than learning and trophies above grades. Only among the lower-school cadets who feared my superior rank and age did I feel that being Jewish was not my blinding characteristic.

This latest miscarriage came at the start of that summer of 1949 so I was, in the interim, packed off to my mother's sister Mimi and to Mimi's husband, Uncle Avram. Aunt Mimi had remained childless, never even going so far as to lose a baby. Every year she wrote telling my parents to send me to the South Carolina farm for a long visit. I sensed Aunt Mimi wanted me to be a son to her and Uncle Avram and I was curious to try out the position.

Unlike my mother, Aunt Mimi was a big woman, yet not inclined to smother. She wasn't a toucher but a watcher. I'd be mowing the grass around the little gray shingle farmhouse and look up to find her dark eyes following from one of the small windows scattered unevenly over the gray.

I thought back then that Uncle Avram saw me through his wife's eyes too. Every morning at breakfast he would list my chores for the day. Over lunch, whether I had completed the list or not, he would review my work, correcting and complimenting, and then say, "Ask your Aunt Mimi if she needs you." Only after she would shake her head no would Uncle Avram proclaim, "Enough for one day. You play now. A boy only grows while he's playing."

At first I resented being released even more than I resented any of the chores. I didn't know how to play outdoors. The sounds of crickets and cicadas would overwhelm me when I was alone and aimless. I wanted to retreat to the shelter of the house but I knew that reading would not satisfy Uncle Avram's notion of growing play. Disgruntled, I would set out for the woods with General Patton, the one-eared farm dog, to hunt down gangsters.

"You look more bone than meat," Uncle Avram clucked a few days after my arrival, as if assessing my ability to lift tractors. "Still, you have a man's hands. Here," he said, shoving a cumbersome paper sack into those hands. I opened the bag and stood speechless. I knew he was waiting for some expression of appreciation but it was all I could do to stop myself from saying, "Thanks anyway." Inside the bag were a hammer, a small handsaw, and a box of threepenny nails. "It's a start," he said, suddenly awkward.

"You want me to make you something?" I said ungratefully.

"I want you should make you something," he said as he walked away.

In the spare room I crumpled the bag and shoved it under my bed so it would be out of the way.

} {

One still afternoon in late June, I watched a black man come down the empty road and stop at the gate leading to the farmhouse. General Patton commanded his attention. Dogs, unlike cats, take note of color, have prejudices and preferences often inexplicable to their masters.

The General ordered an about-face. The man shrugged, unfastened the latch, and hoisted a small sack over his right shoulder, out of dog range. When the man entered the yard, the General crouched low to the ground and showed his teeth. The visitor marched down the path with dog breath at his ankles.

I thought he must have been either very brave or very stupid. The General did not look like the purveyor of empty threats – the ragged flesh where an ear should have been served as character reference. I wondered why my uncle or my aunt, who surely heard the barking, did not call the dog.

When the man, tethered inches from General Patton by invisible chain, arrived at the back door, Uncle Avram appeared. "Here, General," he said quietly. The dog danced briefly, then grudgingly sat at my uncle's feet. Uncle Avram reached down to stroke General Patton's head. "What can I do for you?" he said with measurable politeness.

"Well, suh, I thought maybe I could do something for you, and your missus, and your boy here." He swung the sack down from his shoulder and drew out a beautiful plump hen. "Fresh killed this morning. Meaty as they come."

"No, thank you," said Aunt Mimi, even more chillingly polite than my uncle.

"I'll give her to you for a good price."

"We raise our own chickens," Uncle Avram said.

"Not fat as this." The man turned his prize round in the sunlight so it could be admired from all sides.

"No, thank you," Aunt Mimi said again.

"She's a steal," he tried once more. "I need me some cash," he switched from salesman to shnorrer. "Medicine for my boy, about the same age as thissun."

The switch did not help his case and it released my aunt and uncle from the bonds of civility. They said nothing.

The man shrugged as he had on the road while calculating the danger from the dog. He eased the hen back into the sack and returned up the path without any more polite words to mark his departure.

"But, Aunt Mimi," I said when the man once more stood on the far side of the gate, "I thought you needed all your hens now for laying."

"That's so," she said and disappeared into the house.

I followed Uncle Avram down to the shed where he began sharpening an axe blade. The shriek of metal on stone silenced me. I was about to turn away when my uncle said, "Use your head, Alan."

I tried to understand what it was he wanted me to understand. I was sure it had something to do with color or religion and I was afraid of exposing my ignorance, or theirs.

"What can you say about that man?"

"He was a Negro."

"He was a very scrawny Negro." He slowed for me but, as I showed no sign of catching up, he went on. "This Negro was all bones and sinew. Good for the soup pot, maybe. So what do you expect he should do with a very fat chicken? He should do us a favor? He shouldn't. He didn't."

I still couldn't follow the conspicuous trail. "He stole it?"

"Then he'd have eaten it himself, put a little meat on his own bones, or his boy's, if he's got a boy. Stolen meat is the most tender."

"I don't know," I said, weary of the puzzle and of my uncle's pleasure in it.

"He didn't kill the chicken, Alan. It died on him. He turned around and saw his prize hen lying in the dirt, the other hens pecking at it. You don't suppose he would feed diseased chicken to his sick boy? Alan, never eat a chicken unless you see it killed."

That was an important rule, I could tell. So important that I didn't know if it had applications beyond the poultry trade or if it simply stood by itself like: Never take shelter under a tree during an electrical storm.

"What about on Long Island?" I challenged.

"On Long Island," my uncle said as if the distance were immeasurable, "on Long Island you never eat a chicken unless you know the butcher. And his rabbi."

} {

By the end of the second week I sometimes missed the dinner bell, so absorbed was I in hammering my tree house, building my own shelter among all the flying, running, crawling things. After days of scouting with the dog, I had picked the best tree – not the biggest or the nearest, but an old sugarberry with two tiers of strong branches.

One afternoon, when Uncle Avram asked my aunt if she needed me, she nodded and I sulked. I had planned to make a rope ladder for the tree house to replace the boards I had nailed to the trunk. No longer hoping for the appearance of diverting strangers, I was eager to secure my summer against intruders.

Aunt Mimi asked that I deliver the blanket she had been embroidering for Mrs. Nagy's new baby. The Nagys' farm was more than two miles by road, but less than one through woods and over fields. I had never been to their house, but I had been that far with General Patton. I set off with the dog, with the battered canteen Uncle Avram had used in Normandy, and with the blanket, wrapped in brown butcher paper and tied with green twine.

When I arrived at the Nagys' house, I stood uneasily on the rough fieldstone walk. A generous front porch spilled around the narrow three-story frame building, but the steps were broken and the white paint blistered and peeled.

I was trying to decide if I must explain myself beyond my errand – my plan to become a newspaper crime reporter came to mind – when the screen door filled with a woman with several small children clinging to her. "Hello there," she called. "And who are you? Why, I bet you're Mimi's sister's boy from New York. My, were you this tall when you left home or has it been the fresh air and your aunt's good cooking?" The door swung open as Mrs. Nagy called over her shoulder, "Catherine Ann, come and meet a young man who's been to the top of the Empire State Building. Joanie, you go in and pour him a nice glass of that orangeade I've got chilling. Now sit right down and tell us about yourself." Mrs. Nagy patted the porch glider next to her.

I hadn't heard so many words in my three weeks on the farm. Even though I thought Mrs. Nagy would be interested in crime reporting, it didn't seem that I could speak.

"What's your name?"

"Alan," I managed.

"Catherine Ann," she said to the girl who had taken her place behind the screen, "this is Al."

"Alan," I said.

"To look at me," Mrs. Nagy said, but I wasn't looking at her, "you'd never believe I was old enough to have a sixteen-year-old daughter, would you?"

Catherine Ann came out onto the porch. She was throat-achingly beautiful. She had long blond hair streaked with colors I didn't have names for. She had violet eyes. She had breasts. "Hello," she said. She was holding a baby on her hip as if she had been born to it.

"My aunt asked me to bring this," I thrust out the package as though I expected the baby to take it off my hands. Catherine Ann smiled the smile of an older woman. She had small, even teeth and large, high breasts.

Mrs. Nagy unwrapped the blanket. "Will you look at this? Have you ever seen anything so pretty? It doesn't seem right to get spit-up all over it. Your Aunt Mimi is a wonder. It's an amazement to me how you people find such time what with having to slaughter your stock just so, and keeping those different sets of dishes, and not being able to turn on your electric lights of a Saturday. Just look at these tiny stitches. Your aunt ought to have a baby or two of her own to do for. Better yet," Mrs. Nagy chuckled, "she ought to have one or two of mine."

I already had ideas about which one I wanted Aunt Mimi to take in. "Thank you for the drink," I said. "I'd better be getting back." I hated my tongue for saying that, but no other words would come.

"Mama, can I walk Al part of the way back?" Catherine Ann took a stray lock of hair and tucked it behind her ear.

"Can't see why not. Put the baby in the crib. Just be back in time to shell the peas for supper. I don't want to have to send your brother after you."

As she climbed over the fence, I saw the rounded tops of Catherine Ann's breasts. "You tell me about New York City, Al," she said.

"Alan," I said. I told her about the subway and the public library and Central Park. I told her about ice skating in Rockefeller Plaza – I didn't tell her I had never done it myself.

"New York must be so exciting," she sighed.

"Yeah, it's really great," I said, sunning myself in the reflected glory. "You should go there."

"I'm going to," she said. "Two more years."

"Are you going to go to college there?"

She shook her head.

"What will you do?"

"I don't care."

I took her to the tree house which was only three Long Island blocks from the Nagy farm.

"This is sure nice. Did you build it all yourself? Look, no one can even see us from the ground unless they're standing right under." She kissed me on the lips. "Let's write letters to each other and leave them here, like a post office."

I tried to kiss her again before she left, but she said once was enough for our first time. My feet didn't graze the pine needles as I floated back to the farm.

The next day I zipped through my chores and barely tasted my lunch. "You are sick maybe, Alan?" Aunt Mimi asked.

"No," I said, "I'm fine. Call me Al," I said.

There was a note waiting at the tree house. Mysteriously, S.W.A.K. was written across a lip print on the envelope flap. The note asked what I was thinking about at that very moment. I replied with the first of our Hot Letters and waited there until she came to collect her mail that afternoon.

Catherine Ann managed to get away to the tree house almost every day. We soon went beyond single kisses to necking and then strategic hand maneuvers. Sometimes Catherine Ann would say that the air was very hot. Then she would take off her blouse and hang it over a nearby branch and I would touch her breasts inside their white cotton brassiere; she would let me unfasten the hooks and out they would tumble. My hands and her breasts never tired of each other.

} {

I wasn't sure if Aunt Mimi or Uncle Avram guessed the turn my afternoon play had taken. Aunt Mimi just watched me as before but I suspected them both of suspecting me. One day at lunch Uncle Avram said, "A boy who has learned to be careful about chickens is a boy who should have learned to be careful."

I waited for the end of the sentence.

"You will pass the horseradish, please, Alan."

I could barely recall the boy who had trailed after gangsters with General Patton. I couldn't believe that boy had ever accompanied me to the farm, raced through these woods, or built a tree house for any purpose other than the one for which it now seemed to be made.

One day Catherine Ann and I sat watching a wren that had home-steaded the sugarberry before me. The bird dropped the remains of a caterpillar from its beak as human cries cut through the forest. Still closer fell the sound of running feet and snapping branches. Accustomed to our presence and disdainful, the wren jerked its head to the side and looked past us. The scrawny chicken man was pounding toward my tree.

"I know him," I whispered.

"Go on," Catherine Ann said. "What kind of business you got with him?"

"I know him," I insisted. "I ought to drop the ladder for him. Something's going on. Look. They're chasing him."

"You crazy? That's my brother Michael back there. They're just having some fun. But if Michael finds out I'm up here, he's gonna turn real serious. He may be a year younger than me but he's lots stronger than the two of us put together. Be still now." Minutes later more foot-steps, many more footsteps, passed beneath the tree and then the quiet closed over us again.

That afternoon Catherine Ann, hot and sweaty and excited, consented to peeling away her seersucker shorts and cotton under-pants. I turned her, belly down, upon the picnic tablecloth I had taken from Aunt Mimi's linen closet.

I had expected intercourse to be much more complicated and not so habit-forming. For the next two weeks Catherine Ann would climb the rope ladder, remove all her clothes, present her beasts for their share of attention and then lie upon them, firm and swollen, as I entered her after the fashion of the dogs I had watched in New York and the animals around the farm. When one day, after playing with her nipples, I held Catherine Ann's shoulders to the floor of the tree house and came into her from the front, we stared at each other. I nearly fell over myself on the way back to the farm, swaggering with self-satisfaction – we thought I had invented doing it face-to-face.

I was bursting to tell someone. For one lunatic moment I thought of crowing to Uncle Avram. Instead, I took apart the old chicken coop he never got around to and stacked the broken boards by the kitchen woodpile for kindling.

The next day Aunt Mimi went into town and was late coming back to fix lunch. Then she had to make me some spice cookies. I held half a dozen of them, still warm from the oven, in my hand as I tore through the pines. General Patton began yelping as we neared the tree house. I told the dog to quiet down but he ignored me.

"Sit," I ordered, irritated now.

He stood still but continued barking. Suddenly from nowhere a tree limb caught the General along the side of his head. Another tree limb came down upon my shoulder, sending me sprawling to the ground. I thought the old sugarberry had come alive, was paying me back for the nail holes and the gouges. Then there were feet and hands and voices and, finally, faces. Someone was kneeling on my shoulders and the pain colored everything yellow.

"Don't you ever go near her again." He was blond, too, with the same violet eyes. "You hear me, Jewboy?" A foot detonated between my legs.

I had a broken collarbone. General Patton lost an eye. Aunt Mimi said, "Who did this to you?" but I didn't answer. Not because I wanted to protect anyone, though I hoped that's what she'd think – I didn't know how to explain myself to those quiet, dark eyes.

There was almost a month left of my stay. My father wired that he was taking my mother to the Adirondacks for her health and I could join them if I chose. I decided to stay put. I wasn't surprised when Catherine Ann never visited or inquired after me. After two-and-a-half weeks I stopped wearing a sling and resumed some of my chores, but I passed the afternoons by reading outdoors in a corner of the yard, out of the view of any windows. I no longer spent time at the tree house. Occasionally I walked through the woods with General Patton, but now I always carried a gnarled and knobbed walking stick and I always paid attention to the General. I decided I didn't want to be a crime reporter.

One day I brought my tools, the ones Uncle Avram had given me and a few I had bought for myself, and slowly dismantled the tree house. With my good arm, I remembered to check the hidden fold in the trunk that served as our mailbox. My last Hot Letter, written those long weeks earlier, had been removed with nothing left in its place.

} {

My aunt and uncle settled me on the train for New York with a box lunch crammed with small packages done up in brown butcher paper and tied with green twine. Aunt Mimi kissed me quickly, leaving a patch of damp on my cheek, and was out again upon the platform. My uncle stood over me, waiting. I shivered in the shade of him.

"Uncle Avram," I said before I knew which words were pressing to come out, "what happened to the chicken man?"

"Chicken man?" He turned the phrase over in his mouth, tasting it.

"You know. The Negro who tried to sell you the dead chicken."

He shrugged. "I hear nothing about him." I could feel his eyes, like Aunt Mimi's, searching me. "I would hear if something very bad happened."

He must have seen through to the relief I was masking for he patted my shoulder repeatedly. From the vantage of all these years later, I have to wonder if he spoke the truth or if that reassurance was his parting gift to me.

"So," he said, "this is the summer you lost your innocence." I thought he was still talking about the chicken man. "Now I have something to ask you, Alan. Did you love the girl?"

I was surprised by the question, surprised he thought me old enough to answer it, and then surprised I had no answer to give.

"No?" he said. "Not love. Ah well, then you did not lose enough. You are still young," he comforted himself. "There is time. Maybe next summer, eh?"

But there would be no next summer for Uncle Avram. Later Aunt Mimi wrote that the doctors at the hospital said he had been burdened with an enlarged heart. I could have told them that.

He was buried two towns away, where there was a Jewish cemetery. Right after – even my mother was surprised at how fast – Aunt Mimi sold the farm and left for California.

} TRANSUBSTANTIATION {

Martin and Janet had been married for twenty-nine years, three months, and seventeen days when their car was attacked by two teenaged boys. Perhaps only one was an attacker and the other served as audience, but Martin and Janet saw two youths standing on the curb giving each other a high-five as the rock sailed through the open window on the passenger's side.

Janet didn't see anything at all after that, not until four days later when she finally regained consciousness.

Martin hadn't been injured but you wouldn't know that to look at him. He remained at Janet's bedside in the hospital day and night.

Their two sons flew back to Duluth to be with their mother, but both seemed to have a hard time staying more than a few minutes in her room. Paul, who had waited until he was settled in Minneapolis before telling his parents he was gay, kept going off on shopping expeditions. "Need anything while I'm out, Dad? How about a new shirt? I owe you a birthday present."

The first time, he came back with a vase of purple irises to enliven the still, neutral room. Martin thought that, unless Janet awakened soon, the irises would be wasted. He thought the time to buy flowers was when she was sitting up, able to appreciate them. He thought much the same about the candy, book, nightgown, magazines, bath oils, videotapes, and perfume Paul returned with. He wondered what the staff thought when they maneuvered around the purchases collecting on the bedside cabinet. It embarrassed Martin to have this pile of presents accumulating for a silent, sleeping woman, as though he did not understand the gravity of the situation.

Brian, their other son, the one who lived in Boston, spent more time smoking outside the hospital than waiting in it. Unlike his brother, he was unflaggingly interested in the opposite sex and he had discovered the little roof garden where many of the nurses went to smoke.

"Hey, Paul, you should try the roof," Brian said. "There's some male nurses up there too."

Martin found it ironic that so many hospital workers were smokers, a much greater percentage than in the population at large it seemed to him.

When Paul was not off searching for the perfect gift and Brian was not pursuing his dual passions for cigarettes and women, the two could be found somewhere together, having a meal or a cup of coffee, or a drink or two. At least they get along with each other, Martin told himself.

"Dad, why don't you join us this time?" Paul said. "We'll eat downstairs. You can leave word at the nurses' station that you'll be in the cafeteria in case anything happens."

"I'll wait here. You two go on."

They brought food back to the room for their father. He wondered really why they had bothered to come at all.

Martin spent those days and much of the nights remembering. He was so proud of Janet's accomplishments. His income had never been large and Janet had been, as she called herself, a stay-at-home mom, but Martin had often said that Janet saved him more money annually than he could hope to earn. Except for groceries, he supposed she never bought anything retail. She shopped at thrift stores and rummage sales and auctions and garage sales. She had taught herself to sew and upholster and paint and refinish. She baked their bread and tended a bountiful kitchen garden, putting up gallons of tomatoes at the end of the season. She was his old-fashioned girl, Martin would say, beaming.

When Martin looked at his two grown, restless sons, he thought back to how carefully she had dressed them. When Jacob Grueneberg had closed his tailoring shop, Janet had coaxed from him his remaining bolts of dark summer-weight wools, from which she fashioned a series of sports coats and suit pants and vests for Paul and Brian. They always looked like they had stepped out of a store window, wrists never dangling awkwardly, adolescently, below their sleeves. Some people who could guess Martin's salary supposed, looking at the way the boys were turned out, that Janet had inherited a little money somewhere along the line.

The secret to her success, Janet explained to Martin, was the fabric. "See, hon, I can mix and match the patterns. They're so subtle. That Grueneberg bought quality," she congratulated herself.

Martin kept thinking about how proud she had been of the way those boys had looked and how proud he had been of her handiwork. He wondered if the boys thought much about the clothes she'd made for them. Probably not, though both were still smart dressers. He noticed some of the nurses eyeing Paul as well as Brian. Becky, Martin's favorite because she always softly explained what she was doing even if Janet couldn't hear, tried to time her visits to catch Paul in the room, which wasn't easy.

"Didn't I go out with you once in high school?" she blurted as he passed the door.

"Not him," Brian laughed. "He wasn't out in high school. You must have the two of us mixed up." He tried to put an arm around her shoulder but she pushed the clean bed linens she was holding into his embrace instead.

Martin thought it would be a lot easier on everybody if people just wore labels. When he'd been in high school it was said that any guy who wore a yellow shirt on a Tuesday was advertising his particular sexual orientation, so of course nobody in his high school wore yellow shirts ever. But the nurses would probably appreciate knowing right off that Paul was homosexual. The common parlance, "gay," made Martin shudder for some reason. And how would Brian's tag read in the vernacular? "'Horny,' I suppose," Martin mumbled to his sleeping wife and shuddered again. Not for the first time, he marveled that their union, his and Janet's, had yielded such exotic, intemperate fruit.

The doctors had told him the first twenty-four hours were crucial. If Janet didn't regain consciousness within that period, her odds of doing so were greatly reduced. She had suffered brain damage – that's why she was unconscious – but the extent of the damage was anybody's guess. Martin hoped her doctors were much better at caring for his wife than they were at reassuring her husband.

When the first twenty-four hours passed and Janet had not stirred, Martin put all his energy into willing her to move. The doctors said that even if she did awaken she might be permanently paralyzed by the blow. Martin could not imagine those busy hands eternally idle.

By some stroke of luck, both sons were in Janet's hospital room when she regained consciousness. "Two miracles," Martin later said to Becky, shocked that he could summon up sarcasm about such a moment. "My wife awoke and Paul and Brian were actually in the room." He wanted Becky to know she could do better. At least, the father comforted himself, Janet could believe their sons had been patiently there for her, as she had always been for them.

She awoke, she said, with a crushing headache, which any movement exacerbated, and her vision was disturbed, tiny bursts of light shooting randomly through her field of sight like comets across the sky, but her speech was unimpaired – her first words were "You look terrible" to Martin – and the doctors said most of the neurological signs were good. But Martin could see that her responses to their pricks and probings were not uniform. Her reflexes on the left side of her body seemed delayed, as though there were a messenger in her complex nervous system who repeatedly strayed from his desk.

It was going to be a long haul, the doctors confirmed. Paul and Brian congratulated their parents on coming through the ordeal – "Let us know if you need anything" – and congratulated each other on sharing the burden – "Could have been a lot worse" – and packed their bags and left.

Janet spent another week in the hospital. Martin slept at home most nights now but found he didn't sleep any better alone than he did in the chair beside her bed. He took his remaining vacation time and then a short leave of absence from work so he could spend his days helping with Janet's rehabilitation. Martin worked with the physical therapist who said she believed it was his dedication that would prevent Janet from remaining disabled. The recovery process was slow but Martin never despaired, not even when Janet did, because he could see the progress was steady.

"Recovery is the right word," Martin reassured her, resolved that she would recover the person she had been before those horrible boys had launched the missile that had exploded their lives. Every day he pushed her just a bit beyond what she could do. Even in the little things. He never handed her a glass of water, but set it nearby to make her reach for it. He would never give up on her, not even if she begged him to.

His efforts paid off. Janet regained all her mobility and her old determination. Martin could quit thinking of her as his patient and start thinking of her as his wife. But Janet didn't stop there. Just as she hadn't been satisfied with sewing until she conquered tailoring, she was not going to settle for less than complete mastery over her health.

She persisted with the exercise program that the physical therapist had designed for her until she no longer found any challenge in it, then she joined a health club. "A club for healthy people," she laughed when she told Martin. Martin was surprised. Janet had always disdained such enthusiasts in the past. She used to say exercise was boring and unnecessary if one lived an active, full life.

Martin thought this whim would be short-lived. Instead, little by little, it became all-consuming. At first Janet attended aerobics classes, then she got herself assigned a trainer for weight lifting, and finally she took up running. Each time she reached her goal, she would set a new one for herself, as Martin had done for her while she was recovering.

Janet said, "It's really amazing. Instead of feeling exhausted, all this exercise is giving me energy I've never experienced before. I feel so incredibly alive." But apparently she put all of that energy back into more exercise, feeding the machine she had become, like a gambler returning her winnings to the hollow of a slot machine.

Martin said nothing. He understood how a nightmare such as the one from which she had awakened could engender a preoccupation with wellness.

Martin took over the cooking as Janet felt she no longer had time for that and he was worried that she ate so little. She had lost weight in the hospital and now seemed intent on losing even more. He could see she was thinner but he would not have known she had gone from a size 12 to a size 8 without her telling him.

She said, "Nothing fits any more," and it was obvious to Martin she wasn't complaining. Magnanimously, he suggested she alter only her favorite outfits and then go out and buy as much fabric as she wanted for her new wardrobe. Janet looked at him with an expression he couldn't define and said, "I don't have time to sew a new wardrobe. I'm going shopping."

A little furrow of anxiety settled between Martin's eyebrows when he would think of the money they owed in hospital bills – they had 80/20 insurance coverage – and the additional expenses of Janet's health club membership and store-bought clothes. But she had made do or made over or made new for so many years he could not begrudge her a measure of frivolousness now.

Her new wardrobe was different. It wasn't just that she wore smaller sizes. In fact, the odd thing was, even though she was thinner now,

Martin felt her body somehow took up more space. Certainly he was a lot more aware of it. In the past when she dressed casually, Janet had pulled on a pair of slacks with a matching top, an outfit that could take her just about anyplace except a wedding or a funeral. Not that she had dressed all that casually all that often. Most of the time she'd worn skirts or dresses with their coordinating jackets. Janet had always been justifiably proud of her jackets. "They give an outfit a finished look," she used to say. Now when she dressed casually, it was in some combination of clinging fabrics in electric colors and hallucinogenic patterns that seemed to scream in protest against being worn together. Instead of the careful coordination that had marked her appearance before, Martin decided that she now wore her clothes in juxtaposition, if there were such a thing.

It also seemed to Martin that these clothes couldn't take her anywhere except to the health club, but she wore them unself-consciously around the house or to the store or to restaurants where she lunched with people she had met while riding a stationary bike. She had a new circle of friends who dressed the same way, grown men and women who wore tight sausage-casing bike shorts when nowhere near a bicycle.

But Janet still liked to dress up as well. Her favorite new dress had an oval cut-out over the chest. On another the back was made up of a crisscross of flimsy straps. Another was slit all the way up to her thigh. All the dresses looked unfinished to Martin. As though the seamstress had run out of material very near the end.

He couldn't help but notice that each of the fancy outfits Janet bought now was black. Gone were the floral print dresses with their coordinating jackets in bright solid colors. Literally gone. She had boxed them up and dropped them at the St. Vincent de Paul store, cutting out the labels that read "Handmade by Janet Hagen."

Martin had suggested she hold on to the clothes for a while. "Who knows – you might grow back into them," he'd said.

"Not on your life," Janet had snapped back. "I'm not ever going to look like that again."

Martin was confused. He felt somehow her words were a criticism of him.

He watched her. He had always been unsettled by people who remade themselves. A man they had known from church became an Orthodox Jew at the age of thirty-five. A girl he had dated in high school later changed her names, all of them, from Mary Magdalene Potter to Molly Bloom, without benefit of a husband. People who invented themselves, who didn't accept the name or religion or political party they were born into, fascinated Martin like fire fascinates a nine-year-old boy. He had always seen the danger in it.

Paul and Brian were delighted by the transformation of their mother. "The New Woman," they saluted her. Martin had thought they might be resentful. She no longer fussed over them or gently interrogated them about their lives. They were welcome to join her on her latest adventure – or not. It was up to them to choose. Martin thought it strange that they spent more time with their mother now that she seemed to care so much less. Now it was Martin who tried to get everyone to stay home and enjoy a family gathering, but he discovered the old alliances had shifted. No longer were Martin and Janet huddled for warmth against the coolness of their impeccably turned out sons, but rather a singular Martin sat apart, observing these three glossy, dazzling beings who were, at base, unrelated to him.

Their thirtieth wedding anniversary passed quietly. After much deliberation, Martin gave Janet a gift certificate to Nordstrom's. Janet gave Martin a gift certificate for one hour with the massage therapist at the health club. "It will do you good," she promised.

As he did every year except last, when Janet was still too weak for him to leave, Martin flew to Chicago to attend an annual trade show. He had always disliked these conventions, these disruptions of domesticity. This year Janet had proposed accompanying him. At first he had been surprised. She had invariably resisted the possibility in the past, but he knew now the past and the present were unconnected. He had adjusted himself and looked forward to her coming, hoping for a second honeymoon, or rather a first with this new woman. At the last minute Janet changed her mind, declaring the perfect opportunity for a women-only getaway. "We're taking a cabin in Canada up near Thunder Bay. A lot of drinking, talking, and cursing. Just like you men only we won't pretend to fish." But Martin had never gone on such a men-only outing. Except for the annual conventions, he had never left Janet behind.

On the ride from the airport in the hotel van, he realized this was his twentieth trip to Chicago. A milestone of sorts, he supposed. After a long day of listening abstractedly, nodding politely, and grasping hands firmly, Martin made his way down to the hotel bar. It was filled with other conventioneers, men and women in business suits with name tags prominently displayed, and a smattering of women in little black dresses with missing pieces.

His back to the swarm, Martin was sitting at the bar when he felt a hand upon his shoulder. He turned to face Harry McPhee, a buyer he saw year after year at these trade shows. "Martin," he said, "you old son of a gun, how are you?" It was what Harry said every year since they'd met. Then he took a closer look. "Not so good, I see. Tell your old buddy what's up."

Martin looked up at him and saw the concern registered in the creases of Harry's pink brow. He coughed and then took a sip of his drink, trying to clear his throat of the emotion that choked him. "There was an accident," he said slowly. "A year ago last May. Some kids threw a rock. It went through the car window. I wasn't hurt but it...struck Janet." His chin dropped to his chest. "I," he said, struggling for the words to tell Harry, "I lost my wife."

"God, Martin. I'm so sorry. The bastards. The goddamn little bastards. Shit. I knew there was something wrong when you didn't show up here last year. I promised myself I'd call you in Duluth and find out what was going on and then, like the jerk I am, I forgot. Shit, Martin. That's terrible."

Martin nodded. "Twenty-nine years we were married."

} OVER EASY {

Last night I was back in my mother's kitchen eating her thin, rolled-up pancakes while my father was singing "It Ain't Gonna Rain No More" somewhere offstage. I was just about to push myself away from the table and go look for him when the whole kitchen shook and the table was upturned.

I woke to find the headboard of our king-size bed still shuddering from the aftershock. "What happened?" I said to Paul. I sat up, listening first for a burglar and then listening to Paul. He was making a small whimpering noise.

"It's okay," he said, lying on his stomach. "I'm all right."

"Are you sure?" I was thinking, *He's so young,* and then, inconsequently, *He must have had a seizure.* I said, "What is it?"

"Basketball."

"What? What does that mean: 'basketball'?"

"I was driving in for a lay-up," he raised his arms above his head, his right hand lifting the ball and tipping it over his left. "I must have slam-dunked the headboard."

I could feel him push off from the mattress with his feet. "Did you score?" I said.

"The pain woke me up before the ball touched the rim." He shifted onto his back. "My hand hurts."

"I'll bet. I wonder if the noise woke Alec. Everything shook."

"Just the bed."

"The earth moved for me, darling."

He leaned across the foamy swirls of lace-edged sheeting and kissed my arm. "Go back to sleep."

"Do you want some ice or something? For your hand?"

"No. It'll be okay."

I did go back to sleep but not until I could hear Paul's soft sleep sounds, comforting like the steady hum of a fan – white noise.

} {

This morning in the bathroom I said, "I don't know anyone else who dreams like that. I think it's pretty normal to incorporate external things…"

Paul held his razor – the heavy, old silver metal kind – away from his cheek and nodded, "Like a car backfiring becomes a gunshot…"

"Or when you hit the headboard and in my dream the kitchen table overturned. But people don't physically act out their dreams while they're sleeping. I mean, when I was stuffing myself with pancakes, I'm sure my hands weren't anywhere near my mouth."

"It was a first. Playing basketball, I mean. Almost all the dreams I remember are about being in transit – missing trains or losing luggage – but maybe I dream athletic dreams all the time and just don't know it because I don't wake up in the middle of them."

"But what if you had violent dreams like I do? You know, of people chasing you, of having to fight someone off."

"How can you stand going to sleep? They have to mean something, those horrible nightmares you have."

"All my dreams aren't horrible. I have wonderful dreams, too."

"Yes. That's true. Poor Marla." He smiled at me in the medicine cabinet mirror, "You never get any rest."

I looked at him, wondering, examining, and then I erased my expression: Paul doesn't like to be looked at. He often looks over the shoulder of the person he's talking to, hoping to encourage her to do the same. "What if you dreamed about skiing?" I said. "Or parachuting? Would you end up on the floor?" I thought, *It doesn't matter what questions I ask him: his answers won't tell me what I want to know anyway.*

} {

Paul padded barefoot into our kitchen – if this were the 1950s, we would call this frugal space a kitchenette – to fix his standard Sunday morning breakfast. The predictability of Sundays sustains me through the week.

Every Sunday morning my ex-husband Jerry comes to take Alec out to brunch. They usually go to a bar on Laclede's Landing that's filled with smoke and hard rock decibels Monday through Saturday, but on Sunday they serve up a string quartet and everything with hollandaise sauce. I am perpetually surprised that a ten-year-old boy who insists I serve his spaghetti sauce "next to, not on" his pasta will tolerate hollandaise. I guess that says something about his relationship with his father. "Have a good time, Eggs Benedict Arnold," I called after him as he flew out the door this morning.

Paul eats two eggs fried with marinated artichokes and Kalamata olives over toast spread with port wine cheddar cheese every Sunday. These are the only eggs he eats. When we go to the Middle Eastern restaurant in a little shopping center across from the multiplex movie theatre and I order flan with caramel sauce for dessert he always says, "You're not really going to order that, are you?" And when the wife of the husband-wife team that operates the restaurant brings the flan to our table he says, "You're not really going to eat that, are you?" And when I eat it he shakes his head and says, "That's poison. It will kill you." About then I feel the creamy custard sliding out of my digestive tract and puddling in my veins. Paul's Sunday breakfast eggs somehow don't count as cholesterol intake. They don't register; they just pass through, innocently, like consecrated wine in the bloodstream of an alcoholic priest.

The only breakfasts I eat are the ones in my dreams, the ones my mother used to fix for me.

} {

When Paul said he didn't want to have children, I took it personally at first. Then I realized he didn't mind *my* child, he just didn't want any of his own. I felt reconciled, but I didn't see much point to getting married. I thought he could just go on living with Alec and me. Since there would be no progeny to legitimize, why take the chance on a marriage we might have to illegitimize somewhere down the road? I had thought when Jerry and I married our love would last forever; I wasn't so naïve when I met Paul.

Paul said I wasn't being fair. *He* hadn't ruined my marriage. *He* hadn't proved unsuitable. He deserved, no, *we* deserved a chance. I kept putting him off with arbitrary delays: meeting each other's relatives, a trial vacation with Alec, a stressful situation for him at the architectural firm, or a deadline at the museum where I edit catalogues and brochures. I was afraid he could tell I was stalling and that he would get fed up and disappear. I couldn't bear the thought of dating again, spending uncomfortable evenings with someone I wasn't attracted to, but needing someone to be attracted to me. Still less bearable was the unwelcome vision (so easy to picture) of Paul dating – touching – someone else. His elongated prince's fingers charming someone else's hand.

Once when we were watching a kung fu movie on television (He swore I'd like it; I didn't, of course, but I liked his swearing I would), I got up from the floor next to him to fetch the bottle of zinfandel we had left in the kitchen. His hand reached out and gently closed around my ankle. I stood completely still. His fingers played a little ditty up and down my calf. It wasn't sexual exactly, but I had never been so moved by any other touch. I had to will myself to step away from his hand, to get the wine, to resume breathing.

Paul liked to undress me. Watching his fingers work my buttons and zippers and snaps must be like what other people feel when they watch a pornographic movie. I would become embarrassed as my chest rose and fell like a storm-tossed ship or my heartbeat pounded like machines in a foundry. Surely, I would think, he must see the power he holds over me. I guess I was more intimidated by Paul's touch than I was by the prospect of remarriage.

In a way, the decision to "make it legal" was as much a concession to Florine as it was to Paul. Florine had taken care of Alec until he was old enough to go to extended-day kindergarten. After that milestone had been reached, she came to my house only once a week during the school year—I think she turned herself into a cleaning lady so she could keep her eye on us. She had seen me through my divorce and, while I know she envisions her role as something of a buffer between me and the world, I also know she wanted to be around to serve as a buffer between me and Alec. She thinks I am too protective, too afraid for him of all the things that could go wrong.

Florine knew how much I liked – depended upon – cut flowers in my first marriage: there were bowls of waxy gardenias and vases of decadent, bearded purple irises or white peonies dripping petals or dishes of forced yellow crocuses all over the house. I always kept a little crystal glass on my bedside table with a nosegay in it, a few demure pansies or lilies of the valley. Jerry liked to say to company that living in our house was "like residing in a nursery." And since his pet name for me was "Baby," he especially liked the ambiguity of it.

Jerry and I sold the house in the divorce so I didn't have the garden any more and I couldn't afford the florist. Florine thought there was nothing too tragic about scaling down from the house to an apartment but she did think our going without flowers was more than she and

Alec and I should have to bear. She took to arriving with armloads of glads and huge sprays of lilies. She filled the apartment with roses and mums. I would come back from work and feel I was trapped in a star's dressing room. For months I was poised halfway between delight and dismay. I told Florine that if I couldn't afford flowers I was dead certain she couldn't. She would shake her head, "These flowers don't cost no money nohow. These flowers is a gift from God." I put my foot down over and over again – Florine daintily stepping over it – before I discovered she collected the flowers from a funeral home run by a member of her congregation. After that, I would compliment Florine on her arrangements and, when I heard her key turn safely in the lock, I would pitch the bedside nosegay that now seemed to give off a faint whiff of formaldehyde.

Florine didn't approve of Paul even before she met him. Once he moved into the apartment there was no hope of winning her over. "Why that boy's young enough to be your son, Mmm Marla. What do you want with *two* boys to raise?"

Florine had started out calling me Miz Marla but I felt too much like a plantation mistress who had lost a war as it was. I told her I couldn't tolerate titles and that plain Marla would do. And she told me she had been brought up to show respect for her elders – I am five years her senior – so a compromise of sorts was reached.

"He is not young enough to be my son, Florine. He is only nine years younger than I am."

"*Only* nine years younger than you? I know womens younger than you who got grandbabies. What you want with another little boy?"

"Paul is a responsible adult with a successful career. More successful than mine, I might add. Believe me, he is nothing like a son to me."

"Well, Mmm Marla, first off, I see the harm of him: who's this boy supposed to be to your son? And you best remember, when boys grow up, they *leaves* the womens that *raised* them. And anyway, what you want a boy around for who's prettier than you? Come to think on it, I just don't see the need of him. Since I found Jesus, I haven't needed to mess with any man. The Lord is my father and my brother and my uncle and my best friend. I don't need nobody else."

"Well, some of us do." Florine doesn't look like the type of woman to renounce men. She is very aware of her appearance. We're about the same size so I give her old clothes and I'm always startled to see how they look on her. A navy blue dress that is too tired to go to the office one more time is transformed by a wide red belt and red heels and a collar of beads. It's not so much that Florine looks smart; it's that she looks sure. "What about boyfriend, Florine? I didn't hear you say the Lord is your boyfriend."

She got that look on her face that reminds me of royalty. "Alls I know is *I'm* never lonely."

That hit home, of course, because I was never more lonely than when I was with Paul.

}{

On Sunday mornings *The New York Times* is delivered to the front stoop of our condo. Paul brings that in. I walk two blocks to the corner in front of St. Roch Church where a gray-haired, brown-skinned man sells me the Sunday *St. Louis Post-Dispatch*.

When the weather is cold he nods but says nothing, concentrating on returning his gloved hands to the warmth of the fire in a battered metal garbage can. I never lean forward to look but I always wonder if he feeds the can logs of old, unsold newspapers. On rainy days he wears an olive-green Girl Scout poncho and so does his stack of newspapers. Then he says, "Fit for ducks," and clamps his mouth shut against the rain. I like to think he doesn't say that to everyone. When it is sunny out, his barometer rises and he asks, "How things been with you this week?" and I tell him. Usually it is something about Alec, but he also heard when I got arrested for protesting the street widening of Big

Bend by chaining myself to one of the old elms, and when I inherited the neighbor's three-legged cat, and when Paul and I got married. I heard when his daughter got a job in Kentucky, when his son moved back home from New York, and when his wife was diagnosed with diabetes.

Some Sunday mornings I've been out of town or sick and so I didn't make it down to the corner, but every week that I've gone to fetch a paper he's been there to sell it. He doesn't get vacations or the flu.

} {

After Paul moved in, Florine stopped bringing flowers. Instead she brought copies of her church bulletin. On the inside back page, the pastor publishes some inspirational verse written by a member of the congregation. Florine would leave the bulletin on the kitchen table, where she had formerly left a vase of flowers, folded open to the latest poem. One week she brought a half-dozen copies of the bulletin to the apartment and stuck them all over – on the kitchen table, on the refrigerator door, on top of the pile of magazines in the bathroom, on my bedside table where the nosegay should have been. The title of that week's verse was "There's No Win When You're Living In Sin." I went around the apartment after Florine left, collecting the copies before Paul could see them. He found one inside the microwave.

"What's this?"

"Florine's church bulletin."

"What's it doing in here?"

One of the "rhymed" couplets read

Living in sin you take a chance with your life
lying to Henry, Sam, Willie, and Mike

And Paul, I thought. "You know what a whirlwind Florine is. She probably put it in there for safekeeping when she was cleaning the countertops and then forgot to take it out," I lied. "She always brings me a bulletin," I said. "She thinks the birth and marriage announcements make it easier for me to keep up with the people she tells me about."

"Goofy, but sweet," was his verdict.

"Yes," I said. I felt a rush of panic as I thought of Florine's quiet, continuing campaign to get Paul to move out, marry elsewhere.

We became engaged that night. I told Florine we decided to get married in part because of her.

Florine said she didn't want "no credit now and, thank you so much, I won't be taking none of the blame later."

} {

This morning I was feeling particularly tired as I struggled with the newspaper, crammed with ads and coupons and real estate deals. I was thinking, *I'll never get through all this*, as though it were a homework assignment due first thing Monday morning. I must have looked as sorry as I felt because the vendor gently tucked the paper into my arms as if it were a newborn.

We have never exchanged names during all our other exchanges – I get the news from him, printed and oral, and there is nothing newsworthy in a name. Today he said, "My son is getting these bruises, ugly purple bruises like nothing you've ever seen before. And he's losing weight too. I told him this is what comes of that vegetarian business. I said we need to put some meat – some red meat – on his bones. A smart boy like him ought to know you get your iron from red meat and iron is important or else you end up with tired blood. That's why he's bruising so bad – his blood vessels are all tired and weak. Now, how does a boy who fusses about his clothes and his hair and gives his shoes a spitshine before he goes down to get the mail let himself get so puny, I ask you? This is a boy what takes extra ordinary care of hisself." He bobbled his head from side to side in bewilderment.

My God, it hits me as I walk home, *he thinks his son is the victim only of poverty and racism and the Newt Gingrich years*, but I have deduced from his brief conundrum that his dashing son is gay and afflicted with Kaposi's sarcoma and has come home to die.

} {

I didn't get much sleep last night. When Paul woke me with his basketball playing, it was for the second time. Hours earlier he had first stroked me into wakefulness and then taken my hand and placed it on his erect penis. "Can I interest you in our firm's latest come-on?"

He is less arch when he isn't self-conscious, like the other evening when we were listening to some White House official on the *Lehrer News Hour* assuaging fears about recession with more talk about the "trickle-down" effect. "You mean the 'piss-on-you' theory of economics, don't you?" Paul said politely to the television.

Last night was the first time since our honeymoon in Hawaii that he awakened me to make love.

} {

I was feeling like a nap before Jerry returns with Alec this afternoon. Paul had cleared away his breakfast dishes and spread *The Times* out around him on the futon couch he brought to the condo from his former life. Sometimes I think he is too young to have had a former life.

"I think the newspaper vendor's son has AIDS," I said. "Imagine being black, poor, gay, and with AIDS."

"I'd rather not."

"And his wife has diabetes. I wonder what his daughter's going to come home with."

"That's a pretty terrible thing to say."

"Why?"

"Racism. Class discrimination. Negative thinking. Take your pick."

"You skipped homophobia." I was looking at him too closely, I knew. Sometimes I've thought that Paul is gay, though I've never thought so while we were making love. I haven't said anything or asked anything because I don't know why I think he might be, unless it is that I am afraid that it was more important for Paul to be married than it was for Paul to be married to me. So it occurred to me to wonder if I had brought up the newspaperman's son as a way to bring up something more. "It's just that everything seems to go wrong for that man. He's afflicted. And patient. Like Job."

As Paul goes back to his newspaper I think that perhaps it is just the combination of being male and being nine years younger that accounts for his not picking up on life's clues.

Paul's age made me nervous from the beginning. He said he found himself drawn to women with more experience than he had. I thought, given time, he'd find me wanting on two scores – my lack of youth *and* my lack of experience. But I was so determined not to repeat my mistakes, not to search out another father figure as I supposed I had with Jerry who is six years older than I am and light years more confident. The fifteen years between my two husbands added up to a generation. They had nothing in common – not their music, not their sports, not their heroes. *And not their women,* I've reassured myself.

When I look at Paul – when he doesn't know I'm looking – even after all this time together, I can't believe my eyes. I can't believe my luck. It's like I won the grand prize in a church raffle or the state lottery. I've been given the cherry-red Porsche or an annual check for a million dollars after taxes just for buying a ticket, for being in the right place at the right time.

} {

Paul doesn't read *The Times* for its coverage of international news or cultural affairs. He reads it for the city politics – precinct news, trial reports, graft investigations, corruption scandals. He lived for one year in Manhattan before accepting a job with the firm here. He particularly enjoys scanning the paper for signs of strikes that would bring the city to a standstill. "I think there's a transit strike brewing," he will turn pages eagerly, as though expecting to nose up a truffle. "Trouble with the firefighters," he might predict, or, "The city could never survive another garbage strike."

Paul declines the local paper. He says he isn't the type to protest street widenings and he can always rely on me to tell him how to vote.

We both know that civic duty is not the reason for my loyalty to the *Post*. What lures me down to the corner week after week is the Sunday funnies. My father used to read them to me as I sat on his lap in the big picture window while my mother made Sunday breakfast. I clip some of the strips and sometimes I'll fasten one to the refrigerator with a magnet but usually they just drift through the condo like so much flotsam. Once, in my first marriage, I found a comic strip had made its way down the laundry chute.

I finished the funnies this morning and saw that Paul had been waiting for me. He wasn't waiting for me to hand them over – he never reads the funnies except the ones I force on him.

"I don't know how to say this," he said, and then he said it: "I'm moving out."

} {

After we came back from Hawaii, I wanted to buy a house in the country, a new place for us to move into, as a family, with a yard for Alec, and a studio for Paul, and a garden for me.

Florine said, "I won't be going out to no country place, Mmm Marla. Just so's you understand."

I understood Florine was hurt. We both recognized that I was prepared to abandon her despite all the years of unspecified kinship.

Paul said, "We don't have the time to take care of a house in the country. We can barely keep up with the apartment."

I agreed with him and kept on looking. And then we stumbled across the perfect place, a two-story white frame cottage on eighty acres, mostly woods, with a creek twisting through the back yard. There was a For Sale sign in front when Paul and Alec and I drove past on our way to an auction. "Let's go back and look," I said to Paul. I was pleading with him.

He turned around and parked the car in the driveway, two dirt ruts flanked by grass. We knocked at the door but didn't expect an answer. The house looked as if it had been sewn shut. Alec and Paul rolled up their pant legs and waded in the creek while I inspected the gardens. There were lots of perennials: buttercups, clematis, Missouri primrose, bee balm, a huge bed of daylilies, rudbeckia, mums, phlox – some in bloom, others whose foliage I recognized, and plenty I couldn't identify. Right outside the back door was a small herb garden laid out in neatly bricked squares.

"This place has karma," I said to Paul as we got back into the car. "Can't you feel it?"

"Since when do you feel karma?"

"Since we found this place."

"What's car-muh?" Alec asked. "Is it good or bad?"

"Good karma is good and bad karma is bad," Paul smiled at him in the rear view mirror.

"Thanks, dude," Alec said and punched Paul's shoulder from the back seat.

Sometimes I think Alec thinks of Paul as a brother – a perfect brother who has never beaten him up or bossed him around or broken his things. "Alec, you should never hit someone who's driving," I said.

I telephoned the agency on Monday morning and heard about the eighty acres and set up an appointment to look at the inside of the house. I drove out by myself one afternoon that week, taking time off from work. I didn't want to drag Paul and Alec out there unless I was convinced it was really worth trying to convince them.

The agent was nice enough, a part-timer who chewed on things when she thought I wasn't looking. She chewed on her nails and on the plastic cap of the cheap ballpoint pen she was using to check off items on a list, and she chewed the ends of her long wheat-colored hair. In high school, in classes with alphabetized seating, I sat behind a girl who was always biting off her split ends and swallowing them. I used to wonder how that girl managed not to gag on the hairs as they went down. I wanted to ask the realtor if she ever had hairballs.

The house was partially furnished, she explained. The old man who had lived there had been "removed" by his adult children who had divided the "nicer pieces" and most of the bric-a-brac among their households.

We went in through the kitchen door. A memory of feeling safe, a sort of *déjà vu,* washed over me as the real estate agent pushed open the door. The kitchen was painted a serene pale green with green, white, and yellow gingham curtains at the door and windows. The sink was the naked, shallow old-fashioned kind with exposed plumbing, not dressed with countertop or cabinetry. A maple table stood against one wall and three chairs were gathered round it. "Three," I nodded to the real estate lady. "There's three of us."

She frowned at me a little. She wasn't much for omens.

I could pretty well imagine the rest of the house, the size and contours of the rooms and the taste that had appointed them. I was wondering how difficult it would be to match the existing wall colors so that each room could be freshly, but not noticeably, painted before we moved in. Then the real estate lady opened a door off the kitchen. "This is the master bedroom," she said. I entered while she lingered on the threshold. In the center of the room was an old metal four-poster that had been painted beige. The bed was stripped of linen. Any bare mattress and box spring have a seedy, seamy look to them, so that alone might have accounted for my sudden sadness, but ranged round the sides and foot of this bed were eight or nine mismatched straightback chairs. One of these was the fourth maple chair that had been missing from the kitchen set. For a moment I saw us again grouped around my father's hospital bed, the visitors the only changing decor in a room where even the tame botanical prints were bolted to the wall.

"Thank you," I said to the real estate lady. "I don't think this is going to work out after all. I'm afraid I'm not a good judge of karma." You should have seen her frown then.

So when Paul found the condo a few blocks from the apartment and Alec said it was cool that he got to stay near his friends and Florine said, "I always knew that country business was just talk," I gave up. I gave in. All the walls in the condo are a crisp, unforgiving white.

} {

When Paul said he was moving out, the first thing I said was "To the country?" I wasn't trying to be funny. He said something else but I found I wasn't listening. I was concentrating on my stomach. It had turned over and I was thinking *How can a stomach turn over?* I kept telling myself that I had been through this before and I had survived. But my stomach wasn't fooled. It knew I had never been through this before. Not this. Before with Jerry there was yelling and crying and therapy and reconciliations. And my mother was still alive so I could go home and we could tell each other that we were glad my father had been spared the sorrow.

This was something new, unprecedented.

} {

Once, some Sundays back, I said to Paul, "You really should read the *Post*. There's an article on a Mennonite community I think you would enjoy."

Paul said, "Sorry, won't touch it." He came around behind me and set his hand piggyback over the top of mine, splaying my fingers apart with his. He took my fingers one by one and pressed the tips onto the paper napkin next to my coffee mug, leaving a legible fingerprint with each stamp. "Book her," he said.

} {

"Did you say why?" I interrupted Paul.

"What?"

"Why you're moving out. Did you say?"

"It's not working."

"What?"

"The marriage. It's not your fault."

I had never felt so embarrassed. So stupid. I had thought it was working. I thought we were both getting what we had expected from the marriage. The only explanation for such foolishness was that I had creamy egg custard where my cerebrum should be.

"I shouldn't have pushed you to get married," he said. "I'm just not a family man, I guess. It's a flaw."

"I thought you liked Alec."

"Of course I like Alec. It's not Alec."

"Then it's me."

"No, it's me." He shrugged, "It's the traditions, the rituals."

"The rituals?"

"I don't know. The holiday dinners. The bedtime stories."

"You have your routines." I thought about buying Neufchatel instead of the port wine cheddar for his Sunday toast.

"Routines, not rituals."

} {

When I was little the only eggs I would eat were hard-boiled ones. And only my mother's. Other people's mothers boiled eggs until the white was rubbery against your teeth and the yolk acquired a poisonous green coat and a faint smell of sulphur, or boiled them only until the white became opaque, still gelatinous, somehow quickened into nasty, shimmering living tissue. My mother's perfectly hard-boiled eggs were accompanied by butter-and-sugar sandwiches, the only sandwiches from which my mother ruthlessly cut the crusts. I loved taking a lunch of hard-boiled egg and fingers of butter-and-sugar sandwiches to school. A bite of white and yellow egg, a bite of white and yellow sandwich. The other children were disbelieving of this diet. "It's a family tradition," I told them. And yet I would never serve such sandwiches to Alec.

} {

"My staying wouldn't be fair to you."

I don't get this. I know it isn't about fairness. I'm crying as I say, "Why did you marry me?" and, despite the clenching pain and the tears that I can't stop, I am curious.

"Because I care for you. More than I ever have for anybody." He touches my shoulder and I am trying not to remember how it feels to bury my face in his neck.

I think *I have to ask Florine why he married me.* I wonder if I can hold out until Friday.

} {

A week and a half ago, on Good Friday, I asked Paul if he would like to help Alec and me. We were decorating Easter eggs with Paas tablets dissolved in vinegar and water as I had done with my mother. Paul said, "Thanks anyway," looking at the dark blue bowl holding one dozen white perfectly hard-boiled eggs that Florine had cooked that afternoon. "You guys aren't going to eat those, are you?" he said. Alec looked at him like he was from another planet.

But then neither Jerry nor my father had sat at the kitchen table for this ritual. My father didn't rest his elbows on the sheets of newspaper layered to absorb the drips of dye as he balanced an egg on a tentative wire wand in a cup of color.

When we finished with the Easter eggs I went into the bathroom to wash the newsprint off my skin. The ink does not stay on the paper any more; it only enters the house on paper, then floats where it will. It surprises me that there are any words left on a page.

} {

Paul is clearing out the closets and drawers of essentials, hurrying now to finish before Alec returns. I can't not watch. I lean against the Shaker table on which, by unspoken compact, nothing is ever put and say, "Why basketball, Paul? You don't even play basketball. Jerry plays basketball." I am thinking, insanely, *Did you know the other players? Was it a pick-up game?* "If you had already made up your mind to leave, I wonder why you didn't have one of your dreams about being in transit."

He comes up behind me and puts his arms around me. "We'll always be friends," he says softly into my hair, his breath caressing my neck.

"No thanks," I say, freeing myself. "That's not what I need you for. I can always turn to the Lord for that."

"I think you're probably angry because I made love to you after I'd already made my decision."

He is so young, I think. "I'm angry because I married you and I moved into a condo and I am happy to make love with you in the middle of the night and none of it matters: there's nothing left for me to concede." I am staring at the daisies I bought as I was leaving the supermarket yesterday. They are treading water in a vase on the nightstand. I am tired just looking at them. In Hawaii on our honeymoon, I could never seem to remember on which side you wear the flower when you mean "not spoken for." I take one of the daisies from the vase and tuck it behind my left ear, averting my eyes while Paul considers the carved birch bark box I had given him and then returns it to the dresser.

"Where are you going?" I ask, dizzy, grasping for one sure thing, some fact to hold onto.

"Does it matter?" he shrugs and turns back to his packing.

And so I know it matters very much. My brain pumps *Who is she? Is she someone I know? Was she the work you had to take care of those nights you were late coming home?* but he is spared the customary interrogation. I am paralyzed by the possibility there is a he waiting at the other end of Paul's escape. Then I realize my husband is right after all: the where and the who are beside the point.

} {

I began menstruating before my mother had a chance to prepare me. I was ten years old. "It's normal," my mother said. "It happens to all girls."

Once I was assured that this was not real blood I was bleeding but blood symbolic of womanhood, I became interested in the mechanics of the process. "Eggs?" I said. "Really? With shells?"

"Silly goose," said my mother.

Goose eggs? I shuddered. "Big ones?" I asked, my voice small, my eyes grown huge.

"Little, tiny *invisible eggs.* You only know one has come out when you see the blood. The egg's too small to see."

It was confusing, hard to imagine, even preposterous, but I had never known my mother to lie to me, not even to protect me.

"How many times?" I asked, frowning, trying to pin down something concrete.

"Once a month," she said, sighing, "every month."

"'Til when?"

"What do you mean?" My mother's mouth tightened, little furrows creased her upper lip.

"Until I'm twelve?"

She laughed, but not at me. She put an arm around my shoulders. "That's when most girls start. You're early. It will go on until you're very grown up. Older than me."

I wanted to ask her if she bled but I knew she had already told me so and to pursue it would be somehow improper, so I asked her, "Where do I get the eggs?" as though I might have to remember to stop off someplace between school and home.

"They're in you."

"They are?"

"All of them," she nodded. "All the eggs for your whole life. You carry them with you from the time you're born."

"Until they come out," I said decisively. "One every month."

"Yes," she sighed. "I'm sorry you've started so early. I did too. It means bad cramps," she foretold, "what they call 'female trouble.' It's nothing serious – it's just, well, like a stomachache. You'll get used to it."

But of course I never did. Just as she never had.

I started keeping a journal in high school and had thought I would keep it forever but Jerry had regarded it as something kept *from* him. "Come on, Baby, let me read it," he would say.

"I can't, it's private." I was shocked each time he asked.

"I don't keep any secrets from you," he would magnanimously declare. "Husbands and wives shouldn't keep secrets from each other."

"There are no secrets in my journal, just privates," I would tell him, nipping at his ear or shoulder, whatever was bare and handy.

Sometimes, very infrequently, I would graze among past entries. I was often surprised by my former self – her thoughts and concerns. Occasionally my journal entry consisted of a quotation of someone else's words or a poem of my own. Early in my freshman year of college I had written a staccato verse that concluded *I am a woman/ I hold the eggs/ Handle me with care.*

The night I told Jerry I was pregnant with Alec he made love to me and then tenderly, oh so tenderly, whispered, "You hold the eggs. I'll handle you with care."

"You read my journal," I said.

"There won't be any secrets between us now. That was my only secret: that I read your journal."

I stopped keeping a journal then and I stopped trusting Jerry.

But I have no excuses when it comes to Paul.

I knew I wasn't safe with Paul from the very first day. And so did the prophet Florine. Her view of female trouble has always been wider than my mother's.

} MEET ME {

Deborah's knee protested with each step she took down the basement stairs. She tried balancing the laundry basket on her other hip, but the pain persisted. She was afraid she was going to have to give up running. Another part of herself gone.

Some of the changes were the byproduct of marriage – the loss of autonomy, the compromises in taste. Some were the direct result of Rob's asking her to change: she had given up smoking; she had taken up bicycling. Other changes were harder to pinpoint, or to pinpoint their cause. Did people find her less interesting and attractive simply because she was married now, settled? Because she and Rob had settled for each other? When she was single, and even engaged, she felt the eyes in a room, men and women's alike, appreciating or appraising her. Lately, she felt invisible.

Mechanically, she set about emptying the pockets of Rob's pants. This was one of the changes he'd failed to make to accommodate her. Pens, stamps, his watch, antacid tablets were but a few of the items she had rescued. Kleenex was the worst offender. When it disintegrated in the wash cycle, the bits would be distributed over the entire load in the dryer and adhere like elfin flecks of *papier-mâché*.

She pulled dimes and pennies from his left pocket and a book of matches from his right. A tilted silver cocktail glass with three bubbles rising from it shimmered on the black matchbook cover. On the flip side was printed *Christopher's* in silvery script. Deborah frowned at the object in her palm. She didn't know of a place called *Christopher's*. And why would Rob, the anti-smoking crusader, be carrying matches from there or anywhere? She fumbled with the matchbook and the lid slid open revealing a scrawl of blue ink against the white interior: *Meet me.*

Deborah sat down on the concrete floor amid the piles of laundry. Was he cruising bars? How long had this been going on? Was it just the one woman or was he a serial pick-up artist? Who was this person she was married to?

She thought about how he, more often than she, was too tired or distracted for sex. Now there was a context for his tiredness and for what was distracting him.

Maybe he, too, had never been to *Christopher's* – yet. Maybe the matchbook was her way of choosing the place for their next assignation.

She tried to stand, but the pain in her knee radiated to her ankle.

Suddenly her first suspicion rebounded within her. Cruising bars. What if he wasn't chasing women after all? *Christopher's.* It even sounded like a gay bar. No wonder she had never heard of it.

A wave of nausea hit her. She lay down, her cheek against the cool concrete. Well, the difference in their sexual appetites was accounted for. She had hated him for those moments while she believed he was seeing other women, but now she didn't know what she felt. Revulsion, yes, and anger that he'd deceived her. But pity, too. For the two of them. Her last conscious thought before retreating into sleep there on the basement floor was that they would have to talk about this but she didn't know how and she didn't know when.

} {

When Rob returned from taking the last of their garden tomatoes to his mother, he found Deborah sitting at the kitchen table folding laundry, one leg propped up on another chair and an ice pack draped over her knee.

"What happened?"

"Nothing," she said. "At least nothing I can be sure of." She pushed a stack of his underwear toward him. "I think it's probably the running."

Rob heard the sadness in her voice. He wasn't surprised. Deborah was addicted to running like he was addicted to caffeine. "It'll be okay." He gave her shoulder a squeeze.

"You think?"

"You're doing all the right things."

"That's what I thought."

"Rest. Ice. Just give it a little time."

"You know, I won't be able to go biking tomorrow."

"I guess not." Rob was disappointed. They had signed up for the Labor Day ride months ago. "So we'll go next year."

"We'll see. Anyway, you're going tomorrow."

"Not without you. We'll do something else."

"Rob, I know how much you were looking forward to it. I'd feel a lot worse if you didn't go."

"Are you sure?" he said, already gone in spirit, coasting down a hill on a curving county road.

She nodded. "The one thing I'm absolutely sure of."

The next morning, in semi-darkness, he packed his pannier while she slept – trail mix, wrench, sunscreen, windbreaker. He rummaged through Deborah's purse for the essential gadget, the little can of pepper spray attached to her keyring. Too often he'd been chased by dogs while biking along country roads. He hoped he wouldn't have to use the spray, but he was taking it. Before his fingers found the keys, they hit upon a familiar, disturbing shape. He drew a matchbook from the leather folds. "Shit," he said softly.

She had promised him she'd given up smoking. How could a runner continue to fill her lungs with smoke? And lie to him about it. He hated deceit more than anything.

He looked at the cover. Now she was going to bars without him. Looking for a safe haven for smokers, he supposed, a smoking club with dues to be paid later in the cancer ward.

He wondered where this *Christopher's* was. Near her office probably. That would explain why she was late getting home twice last week.

He flipped the lid and in the dim light squinted at the hasty scrawl. So that's what the late nights were about. And now the farce of the injured knee. She wanted Rob out of the way. She'd have the whole damn day to meet him.

} WITHOUT WINDOWS {

Lydia had developed a sixth sense for adultery – or her other senses, like a blind man's, became heightened in its presence. She could see it in the way an illicit couple stood side by side yet straining toward each other. She could feel it rise off them, like steam. She could smell it, musky and pungent, winter spices simmering on the back of a stove. She could hear it in the cadence behind carefully chosen words. She could taste it in her own mouth, acrid and sweet, the flavor of rust.

She was finding it everywhere. Last week she had gone to lunch with a friend and discovered it right there in the restaurant – a couple so exposed that Lydia would not have been surprised if the other diners had set down their forks to stare. Christine had said, "What's with you today? You haven't heard a word I've said."

Lydia leaned forward. "Christine, do you see those two over there? In the corner. She's wearing a green dress."

Christine turned and craned her neck. "Nooo. Yes. Should I know them?"

"No. I mean, I don't know them. I was just wondering if you notice anything unusual about them."

"I can't say that – yes, they both have widow's peaks, is that it?"

"Lord. No, forget it. I'm sorry."

Two days ago Lydia had spotted it at the Art Institute. She had shared the Beckmann exhibit with a young woman who was standing in front of the *Columbine*, transfixed by the contradiction of the massive forbidding figure with its splayed, welcoming thighs. Lydia moved past as the young woman sighed, her padded shoulders rising and falling. Then a man in a banker's suit and gleaming black wingtips came into the exhibition hall and Lydia saw that the sighs were not for Beckmann.

The man had stolen away from a desk somewhere, from his wife and secretary, unless this was his secretary. The two traveled around the room, speaking in low voices, eyes examining each other, barely sparing a glance toward the walls. Lydia pretended to study a self-portrait of the artist until they passed her and then she trailed behind them, watching.

She touched his cheek and he grabbed her fingers and pressed them to his mouth. Lydia felt flushed and dizzy as she made her way out of the museum into fresh air.

Now this afternoon, as she was leaving the supermarket, she saw a man pull into a space in the parking lot and then check his appearance in his rear view mirror. Lydia's eyes scanned the lot until she found the car with a woman sitting in it. The woman's car was parked at the far end so that there would be no public display of proximity, no guilt by association of automobiles. The woman got out of her car – she was wearing a white tennis dress – and pulled a green sun visor down to shield her face. As Lydia watched them drive off, she found herself sifting through the change in the pocket of her skirt, searching for a quarter. There was a pay phone right there by the store exit. Lydia, who could never remember her own social security number or her license plate number, could not rid her memory of either of Jack's office phone numbers or his home number which she had dialed only that one time.

Why can't we just go on? she would say to Jack. Everyone else does. It's all around us. You must see it everywhere too.

Her fingers closed upon the large coin in her pocket and then released it.

} {

It wasn't so much that she and Craig had drifted apart but that they were just drifting. Unlike many husbands and wives who stray, their interests had grown more alike over time, rather than less. He had learned to enjoy her museums and she had learned to play his golf and so on. Their life together was placid and incidental. Their life apart was equally traditional: Craig achieved success in his law practice; Lydia tended to the needs of Bonnie who was now three, and to those of Craig's eighty-six–year-old grandmother, and to those of the North Shore community in which they lived. Their house, which had held several generations of Craig's family, was regarded by Lydia as another museum she worked to preserve.

Their life together had become so predictable that Lydia had, some months ago, initiated small unsatisfying rebellions, little bursts of anarchy that fell far short of revolution.

"Would you like milk in your coffee?" she asked Craig one morning as though he were a stranger in his ancestral home.

He frowned at her, taking some time before answering, "You know I always take my coffee black," but not questioning why she was so willing to dismiss the past.

When Lydia wanted to discuss the general uneasiness she felt within their marriage, Craig would reluctantly consent, but the discussions were stillborn. In the face of Craig's insistence that everything was fine, Lydia felt like a relic of the Victorian age: overly sensitive, unstable, suffering from some vague female complaint. In fact, Craig showed substantial relief when stories about PMS hit the newsstands and he could attribute her restiveness to something amuck in her own clockwork. Lydia probably would have continued on, taking mega-vitamins for hormonal imbalance and trying halfheartedly to pierce Craig's armor of contentment, were it not for her discovery that Craig was engaged in an affair.

Craig had volunteered his Saturday morning to drive his grandmother to the ophthalmologist. When they returned Lydia said, "What did Dr. Lamberg say about your eyes, Gran?"

"They're just pussy-footing around. Taking their sweet time. She can't tell when they'll be far enough gone so's I can have the surgery. Meanwhile my eyesight is so bad I couldn't make out my own grandson who is six-foot-something and says he was all the time in the waiting room."

Craig colored and said, "I was reading a magazine. In the corner."

"Then that young receptionist must have cataracts too," Gran stroked the loose skin underneath her chin.

Lydia was less surprised that Craig lied than that he hadn't prepared a better alibi. She watched him go over to the coffeemaker, take down a mug from the glass-fronted cupboard, and dip into the pocket of his madras shorts to slip the wedding ring back onto his finger.

Lydia was not angered so much by the infidelity as she was by his falsity. Clearly he, too, had felt a lack, had wanted more, yet he had made her disavow these feelings in herself.

She didn't mention her enlightenment to Craig. She didn't know yet exactly what she wanted to do about it. She was surprisingly incurious about the other woman and she did not want to be propelled into a course of action by the momentum of revelation. Later, after she had met Jack, she was happy for any justification for having an affair of her own.

He had rear-ended her car at a stop sign near Bonnie's school. Lydia was jolted forward – she had not been wearing a seatbelt and was thinking how Craig's concern would find expression in a lecture when Jack appeared at her window.

"Are you all right? God, I can't believe I did that. Are you hurt? Should I call someone? Do you think you can walk? I'm so sorry. What a klutz – I can't dance either."

Lydia began laughing and then involuntarily raised her hand to her neck.

"I'll get an ambulance."

"No. Please. I'm okay. I'm sure of it."

"Looks like whiplash to me."

"It's not that bad, really. If it still bothers me tomorrow, I'll have it looked at."

"I'm not comfortable with that."

"Yes, but I am." Lydia opened the car door and stepped out.

"Where are you going?"

"To look at my bumper."

"I mean where were you headed when I hit you?"

"Oh." She walked to the rear of the car. "To pick up my daughter from preschool."

"And then?"

"Home," she said, climbing back in gingerly.

"All right, slide over. I'll drive."

"Thank you – I appreciate it – that's just not necessary."

But Jack insisted. He said he wouldn't be able to rid himself of the vision of her in pain and stranded on the road somewhere with her daughter. He parked his car on the street and chauffeured Lydia and Bonnie home, and that was how it had begun.

At the house Craig's grandmother offered Jack a cup of tea made from sage and licorice mint from her herb garden – "This will put some stiffening in you" – but Lydia had already convinced him she was improving so he took a cab back to his car. Back to his life, Lydia thought to herself, but later that night he telephoned. Bonnie pounced on the phone and then ran into the dining room. "It's the driving man, Mommy." Lydia told Craig she would explain later but she never did and he forgot to ask. As Lydia left to get the phone she heard Gran say, "Ah, now that reminds me. I think I'll make a pot of tea."

"I just wanted to check how you're feeling." Jack said.

"Fine, really. How did you get our number? It isn't listed."

"I copied it down when I phoned for the taxi."

"You know my address and phone number and I don't know anything about you, except that you're not a lawyer."

"What makes you say that?"

It wasn't a reference to Craig she wanted to say defensively, even though she hadn't told him her husband was a lawyer. "Lawyers never admit responsibility for anything," she said.

"But I am a lawyer. Probate mostly."

That's when Lydia fell in love, deciding love was no more improbable than their first meeting or his profession. She had never learned to flirt and she didn't think she was flirting now. "I'll be coming into the city tomorrow," she said. "If you're free for lunch I could demonstrate that I've survived our collision."

Jack was free for lunch but encumbered for everything else. He was married with a daughter nine months younger than Bonnie.

"Are you satisfied with Highland Preschool?" he asked over lentil soup. "Carol and I are thinking of sending Rachel there next year."

Lydia felt irony pressing in all around her like a sudden change in the barometric pressure.

They talked more than they ate, and they listened. Lydia heard that Jack's daughter was the center of his life. Jack heard that Lydia felt her life had no center.

Lydia touched Jack's sleeve. "Do you remember meeting Craig's grandmother?"

He nodded. "She told me I had the look of a pup that had been weaned too soon."

Lydia laughed, "What do you suppose that means?"

"I don't think it was flattery."

"She lives with us, or we live with her – it's hard to say which. Craig's parents moved to Arizona the year after we were married but Gran couldn't go with them – she had never lived anywhere but that house, not even after she married – so she sold it to us."

"Ah. Looked like a cross between French Colonial and Early Freudian. How old is it?"

"There've been two additions but the original structure was built in 1853."

"You're kidding. I would have thought there was nothing but prairie there in 1853. In fact, I'd have guessed that, except for right along the lake, it was all pretty much prairie until the boom after World War II."

"The really exciting bit is that the house was built for Craig's great-grandmother by her father, Horace. That's one of the reasons I married Craig, I think. The house has stayed in his family so long it felt like a kind of marriage insurance – two fireplaces, a pantry, a porch swing, a great-great-grandfather named Horace – what could go wrong?"

} {

Gran said, "You'd better change your clothes, Lydia. Bonnie and I have a surprise for you."

"Change up or down?" she asked.

"I don't know about that. All I know is you don't want to be wearing any dresses with lace collars on them."

"Maybe if you tell me what the surprise is, I can figure our what to wear."

"We're going to make soap, Mommy," Bonnie burst forth as though uncorked. She pressed her hands together in an attempt to contain her excitement.

"Soap? What do you mean? What kind of soap?"

"Lye soap," Gran smacked with satisfaction. "All our women have made it. You need to learn so's you can teach Bonnie."

"There's plenty of time to teach Bonnie, don't you think?"

"That's as may be but who's to say how much time there'll be for me to teach you?"

"All right," Lydia relented. She would have to phone Jack and cancel her trip downtown. She took Bonnie's hands in her own and pat-a-caked them together. "Gran, why did you pick today?"

"Because," Gran said smugly, having prepared for the question, "because today I finally have enough good ashes stored up."

} {

"I'd like to tour your house someday," Jack said.

"Did I tell you Craig's great-great-grandfather hand-carved the olive branches above the windows?"

But Jack never went to the house again and Lydia never invited him. Instead, when they met for lunch once, sometimes twice a week, she would describe it to him, one room at a time with its furniture and family portraits and memories that had been handed down the generations.

"Listen to yourself, Lydia. Anyone would think it was you who'd grown up there."

"In a way, I did. My father was a robotics engineer so we were constantly moving from job to job. We never stayed in one place long enough to unpack all the boxes, except for Japan. And even there we lived in a small apartment."

"How long did you spend in Japan?"

"From the time I was nine until just after my fourteenth birthday."

"A pretty big chunk of a child's life. You don't think of Japan as home?"

"I miss the landscape and the culture and the people, but they were never mine." She shrugged, "When American girls were experimenting with their mothers' lipstick, I was sitting in front of a mirror putting cornstarch on my face and slanting my eyelids." She illustrated, tugging at the corners of her eyes with her index fingers.

"I've gone back twice for visits," she said. "But those were before Bonnie was born. And I've taken some courses in Asian art. That's how

I got involved at the museum. But my picture of family and friendships and...home came from books. Louisa May Alcott. Gene Stratton Porter. Laura Ingalls Wilder."

"I'm starting to notice a pattern here."

"Old-fashioned? Romantic?"

"Three names per author."

Lydia laughed and then bit her lip, considering. "Not only is Craig's the first house I've ever lived in but it's the very house, complete with family, I read about in all those books."

"What about your parents now? Do they finally have a place of their own?"

"A place, yes. When my father retired, they bought a condo in West Palm Beach."

"Hardly storybook. All right, I'm resigned. Tell me more about the house."

"Gran had three rooms added on during the Depression. She had started out wanting just one more bedroom and indoor plumbing, but labor was so cheap the house just grew. I think she couldn't bear to put the workmen out of jobs."

"I suppose you had a full-time job redecorating when you moved in."

"Me?" Lydia frowned. "Do you picture that as the sort of thing I would enjoy? I haven't even rearranged the furniture. I've reupholstered a few pieces, but they were desperate cases. It's Craig who changed the house."

"Changed it how? You make it sound sinister."

"It was sinister. Craig put a big greenhouse window in the family room. That was the original dining room. Horace had built it without windows as a refuge from electrical storms – I guess that was pretty common – so the whole family would gather in that room at the first streak of lightning."

"What about the basement?"

"There isn't one. I guess they weren't building basements in the 1850s. Or maybe Horace would never have finished the house in time if he'd had to excavate a basement too. I don't know. Anyway, the family room was where Gran would sit and rock in the dark – no lamps turned on, the TV set unplugged – every time there was a storm right up until the glass was installed. Now, practically one whole wall is window so that's the room she's most afraid to be in during a storm."

"Poor woman. What does she do?"

"Wanders through the house, mostly walking the hallways. She's even afraid to go to the bathroom – it's not funny – because every toilet in the house is next to a window. God, I wish Craig could have just left everything the way it was."

"Like a shrine?"

"Like a Japanese teahouse," she said. "No changes made ever."

"Not even for the better?"

She shuddered. "We're not talking about a mouse trap. You don't try to build a teahouse better; you try to build each one the same. Whatever differences there are shouldn't be worth mentioning, or noticing. The wood used for framing is old and scarred so that a new teahouse will look pretty much like an old teahouse. Any teahouse you enter should feel familiar after you've experienced your first one.

"A few years back I went with Craig to a college reunion in Ann Arbor. While he was at his old fraternity house, I visited the Museum of Art on campus. They had a model teahouse as the central feature of their Japanese collection. The label said that two adjectives are typical of a teahouse: *wabi* and *sabi*. They mean 'refined poverty' and 'antiquity,' respectively."

"So you're saying your house is like a teahouse in that it's old and graceful?"

Lydia winced. "I wasn't trying to make a comparison with the house. When I was talking about *wabi* and *sabi*, I was thinking about Gran."

As the waiter approached, Jack pantomimed signing for the bill.

"And what about you and electrical storms? Are you afraid of them?"

Lydia found herself more interesting in the light of Jack's curiosity. "No, I don't think so. And I guess Craig didn't inherit it." She raised her glass and then lowered it again, dipping her finger into the iced water. "Last spring, when we had all that rain and the Des Plaines River flooded, Gran told Bonnie she should hide so the storm wouldn't get her. We found them both in Gran's room, Bonnie under the bed and Gran sitting on the floor between the bed and the wall, holding Bonnie's hand. Craig told Bonnie there was no reason to hide and he took her out on the balcony to look at 'the pretty lights in the sky.'"

"What did Gran do?"

"She told me about the time her older brother threatened to tie her to a tree during a storm. She swung a coal scuttle at him and it caught him on the side of his head. I'm sure she told me the story because she thought Craig was tormenting Bonnie and she wanted me to make him stop. I brought her a glass of milk and she sipped it on the floor there between her bed and the wall, as far away from any windows as she could get." She turned her head slowly as though counting the windows in the restaurant.

"Carol doesn't sleep with me any more," Jack said. "Not since Rachel was born."

"That's a long time," Lydia said.

"Before, I was always trying to solve it – trying to talk it out or rekindle the flame or get her to agree to counseling. Now I'm afraid I don't want it solved."

Lydia wondered, as if she were watching herself from a distance, how long it would be before she and Jack became lovers. She waited to tell him about Craig's involvement elsewhere. She waited because it no longer seemed a reason for her choice.

During those first weeks Lydia neither hid nor revealed her meetings with Jack. She saw him in the most public places but she never seemed to see anyone else she knew on those occasions. Magically, Craig avoided asking her precisely those questions about her day that would have included Jack in the answers. Lydia wondered if that meant he knew, or if he really believed all was as it should be – as it had always been – between them.

But Gran was sensitive to changes. Her bunion signaled a drop in the temperature. Her left hip warned of wet weather.

"Maybe you shouldn't leave Bonnie with me any more, Lydia," Gran said one afternoon when Lydia returned from a meeting with Jack.

"Is something wrong, Gran? Is your arthritis acting up again?"

"No." She lifted her chin.

"Is something else bothering you?"

"Nothing's bothering me," she complained.

Lydia shook her head slightly. "I thought you wanted me to leave Bonnie with you. You were always suggesting it."

"It's different now." The hands in Gran's lap were gnarled and seamed, like tree bark, but her face was unlined, untouched by time except for a soft, powdery finish.

"Different how? Has Bonnie been difficult?"

"Bonnie? No." Gran waved both hands at Lydia, fanning away the suggestion.

"What then?"

"I don't know. I'm too old. Maybe she needs to spend more time with her mother."

"Well, I won't leave her with you. You needn't worry about that any more." Lydia was ashamed to hear the coldness in her voice.

} {

"All right," Lydia said two days later across the white linen of the restaurant table, "I'm ready."

The hovering waiter approached to take their lunch order but Jack signaled him away. "When?" he said.

"Tomorrow," she shrugged. "Today if you like."

"Are you hungry?"

"Not at all."

They left the restaurant for a nearby convention hotel. Jack brought out a credit card at the front desk.

"Wait," said Lydia. She drew three crisp $50 bills from her purse. "I think cash would be better. How much do we need?"

Lydia had known making love with Jack would be different from anything she had experienced because talking with Jack was unlike anything she had experienced.

"Is that how you are with Craig?" he asked her as they lay side by side, their feet interwoven. "I'm sorry. Don't answer that."

"I wasn't going to."

"It was like I've imagined," Jack touched her shoulder shyly as though he had not touched her otherwise.

"I will bear in mind that whatever's said comes from a man who's been celibate for more than two years."

"I didn't know people could be this happy."

"Yes," she said.

"Or this unhappy," he said.

He sent her Frango mints, two dozen long-stemmed red roses, and a bottle of Chanel No. 5.

When Craig saw the roses he said, "Is there a special occasion that's slipped my mind?"

"No," Lydia said and waited for the next question, which never came. She felt a little sorry for Craig's lover who obviously never received long-stemmed roses.

When she next saw Jack she said, "What exactly is it that you're trying to do?"

"Court you. I thought that was obvious."

"But candy, flowers, and perfume?"

"Absolutely. All the clichés. What could be more appropriate?"

"It's just because they are clichés that you're going to get us into trouble. Eventually Craig will have to notice."

They didn't lunch in restaurants or risk the large downtown hotels any more. They found a small hotel on the city's north side where they picnicked in their room on tins of pâté and jars of dollhouse vegetables or cartons of pork fried rice. Once Lydia brought homemade chicken soup in a thermos after Jack confessed to a cold. The day after her birthday he brought a bakery cake with her name and pink rosettes in sicky-sweet icing.

They ate Irish smoked salmon while sitting in a tub of hot water.

"How long can this go on?" Jack said, tempting fate as he licked his fingers.

"Not a moment longer," Lydia said and splashed him. "Or you'll be going back to the office all salmon-pink and prune-wrinkled."

} {

"I think I'd better go with you tomorrow to the Loop," Gran said.

"Oh, Gran," Lydia whirled around, "I was planning to take the train."

"Well, I've been thinking I'd like to get some new Sunday shoes and that bald-headed young man at *Fields'* seems to do the best by my feet."

"Later in the week," Lydia said, "I'll drive you in. We'll have lunch at *The Berghoff.*"

"You're a good girl, Lydia, but I worry about you. At least you don't smoke like some of them," she sighed.

} {

"I want to marry you," Jack said. He had waited until Lydia had dressed again and stood fastening her thin black leather watchband to her wrist.

Even though she had been expecting it, Lydia felt her heart constrict, her breath catch. "Oh, Jack, how can we?"

"Like ordinary mortals. We tell them. We get lawyers, we live through it, and then we live together, until death do us part."

"That easy."

"That hard."

Lydia shuddered.

"Think of it," he said. "Imagine going to the theatre together. Or the hardware store. Especially the hardware store. Spring in Mexico, fall in Greece. Winter in Disney World with Rachel and Bonnie."

"I'd have custody of Bonnie – Craig wouldn't fight me – but you'll lose Rachel, Jack."

"I won't lose her. It will be different, but I won't lose her. Look, I'm not minimizing it – that part is hell – but there's no choice. We have to be together."

"Sounds like a choice of hells."

"We'll tell them tonight."

"No, not tonight," she shook her head. "Craig has a late meeting. It would be impossible. Tomorrow," she said. "On Saturday. There will be more time." She bent her forehead to his shoulder.

"I guess the news will keep for another day."

Lydia flinched and Jack put his arm around her. "It will be all right," he rocked her gently back and forth. "It will be all right."

} {

That night as Lydia stood over the stove stirring bits of apple and onion into brown rice, she wondered how many more times she would stand here, how many more meals she would fix for Gran.

When dinner was finished Bonnie said, "I want you to get a baby brother in your tummy like Jill's mommy."

Gran said wistfully, "I would like a nice bread pudding now and then."

It was past eleven when Craig came home. Lydia surprised herself by succumbing to sleep when she had expected to toss and turn. At one in the morning she was awakened by an explosion – a gunshot or a cherry bomb or maybe just a car backfiring. She left the bed where Craig slept to peer out the window, holding the curtain across her nightdress. The sky was suddenly slashed with white neon, so brightly electric it hurt her eyes. Then the thunder followed like the roar of a subway, propelling Lydia out into the hall.

She opened the door to Gran's room, which was quiet, bereft even of the low machinelike humming that attended Gran's sleep. "Gran," she said, opening the door wider, "are you all right?" even as she knew the room was empty. She hurried now to Bonnie's room, afraid that Gran had needed Bonnie's fear to ease her own. Bonnie's room, too, was empty. She called their names, "Gran! Bonnie! Where are you?" but the only response was Craig's. He lumbered out of the bedroom, out of his sleep, to say, "What in the hell's going on?"

"I don't know," Lydia said. "Gran and Bonnie aren't in their rooms and they don't answer. This couldn't be a game, could it?" Lydia was really frightened now because she no longer knew what she feared except that whatever was happening was somehow her fault: it was she who had brought chaos into the house.

Craig systematically searched the second floor while Lydia covered the first, her panic growing in each succeeding empty room. She caught herself bargaining with God, offering in trade a life's mate for two transitory dependents.

"I've got her," Craig called from the second floor landing.

"Who?" Lydia asked, steadying herself.

"Bonnie. The little monkey was out on the balcony enjoying the fireworks. She couldn't hear you over the storm. Can you beat that? She's Daddy's girl, all right."

"And Gran?" Lydia called.

"I don't know. Bonnie hasn't seen her. Keep looking. What a household," he congratulated himself.

Could the old woman have been obliterated by lightning? Does there come a moment somewhere down the road when one's worst fears are realized? Lydia went outside to check the yard below the balcony. The rain stung her face, obscured her vision. Illuminated by another charge of light, Lydia suddenly remembered the walk-in storage closet in the laundry room, their modern, efficient substitute for a basement. Gran was there, wedged into the small portable crib Bonnie had long ago outgrown. "Gran," said Lydia softly, but the old woman was sleeping soundly in this room without windows. Lydia drew a bath towel from the clothes dryer and laid it across Gran's shoulders.

She told Craig they would have to think of something. They had to make one room safe for Gran.

"This is crazy," Craig said.

"But that doesn't matter," Lydia said.

} {

She dialed Jack's home number at seven in the morning and prayed for Jack to answer.

"Hello?" he said.

"Did you tell her?"

"Not yet." Jack's voice dropped. "She's still asleep. Rachel is going to play group later. I thought I'd tell her then. Are you okay? What did Craig say?"

"I didn't tell him." Lydia waited for something to suddenly change her mind, but nothing came. "I'm not going to tell him. It's not possible."

"Oh God, what happened? I'm coming over."

"No," she said, "that's impossible too. You couldn't stand being a weekend father."

"I can't stand being a weekday lover. Tell me what happened last night."

"The storm." Lydia looked into the mirror that hung over the telephone table in the hall. She saw whose face? – Gran's? – no, her own mother's, tired, hopeless, looking back at her. "If I left, Craig would put skylights in."

} {

They saw each other two more times. On the first occasion Jack tried to get Lydia to change her mind. "Who would get custody of Gran?" she said.

On the second, Lydia tried to get Jack to change his.

"We could go on like before, Jack. It's better than nothing. Does it have to be all or nothing?" She didn't know how to explain to him that she just couldn't be responsible for any more storms.

"Going on is worse than nothing," Jack said.

So she had promised finally that she would not call him again unless she left Craig.

} {

Lydia took the change from her skirt pocket and dropped it into the canister held out by a middle-aged woman standing outside the store entrance wearing a yellow plastic banner draped over one shoulder and a white plastic straw hat with a yellow hatband.

"Thank you for helping cystic fibrosis research," the woman said loudly, prompting other passersby.

Lydia loaded her groceries into the car. She didn't know how long she had stood there in the parking lot. She had an appointment with a young man who would install wooden shutters in Gran's room.

"After the shutters are up," she told herself. "Then I'll call."

} THE RIVER'S DAUGHTER {

Leland burst through the back door flailing his arms like a fractured windmill and shouting, "Oh my God! Oh my God! Oh my God!" altogether reminiscent of an overwound wind-up toy.

I'd known Leland for over thirty years and had never thought him particularly excitable. Bashful, yes, but not excitable. Right after high school he had a brief romance with my sister Carrie and later he became the local John Deere dealer, so Carrie never resists an opportunity to torment him with talk larded with double meanings about plows and earth movers. She says he blushes better than any man she's ever seen – gradually, from the neck to his cheeks and then on up through his ears, like he's just filling up with embarrassment.

"Rein in those horses, Leland," I said. Whatever he had to deliver wouldn't get stale in the thirty seconds it took to wipe Sam's hands with the dishrag hanging over the faucet of the kitchen sink. We had been fingerpainting with chocolate pudding and I wasn't about to hear any earthshaking news until Sam posed no threat to the trellised ivy wallpaper. For her birthday present, Carrie had told me she wanted the whole day to herself so I was babysitting until she came home and I wanted the house to look like it had when she left it.

Leland jiggled in place while I settled Sam on the floor with some plastic measuring cups. I nodded, "You can go ahead now."

Now he seemed agitated in an entirely different direction. "Little pitchers," he said, jerking his head toward Sam and dripping puddles on the clean floor. Then he mouthed something at me that looked like "Hairy goat in thyroid fur."

"Aunt Sissy and Leland are going into the dining room for just a minute," I said to the boy who was paying no heed to us, intent on squeezing the green half-cup measure into the yellow quarter-cup, his tongue hanging over his bottom lip from the effort.

"All right, Leland," I said, laying the thick Sunday *Post-Dispatch* on the carpet for him to stand on, "get it over with quick now. Like a vaccination."

Leland took a sharp breath and plunged the needle. "It's Carrie. Floating in the river. Face down."

I felt the shock of cold river water entering my veins. "How do you know it's Carrie?"

"She had long, dark hair. It was spread out all around her like…like an umbrella."

"Is that it then? All your proof?" I said, my voice rising, sharp and lawyerly in my own ears. "Just the hair?"

"And her shape. Could have been Carrie's shape."

"You finished?"

"No," he drawled, his color rising like the mercury on a thermometer.

"Leland, if you don't tell me everything and tell me quick, I'm going to scream."

His eyes fixed on my grandmother's hooked rug in front of the fireplace. "She was naked," he whispered.

Then it was Carrie all right. "You sure she was dead?" That must have sounded hard, coming from her sister, but I didn't feel hard. I felt like Jello.

"Pretty sure."

"But not *sure* sure?"

"Well, you know how fast the current is by the gravel bar. She got past me."

How could you let her get past you? I hollered inside my head. To hell with Leland. I had to think about what I should do next. I could take the truck and drive round to the Tuckers' place. If she was unconscious, she'd maybe get caught up in that tree there that fell over during the storm. She couldn't be dead. She had nine lives and had barely used up half of them. But I couldn't take Sam with me. No, I couldn't do that. And even in his usual peaceful state, Leland was useless around small children. I had to stay put. And who was I kidding anyway? Face down, he had said.

"I waded in to catch her," Leland said, displaying his sodden pants and boots, seeking absolution.

The only useful thing I could think to do was put down a *Family Circle* and a *Nation* side by side and motion him to step onto those from the wet newspaper. I wondered in a slow-motion way if that meant I was in shock. "Did you at least call anybody?"

"On my cellular fishing pole? I just ran up here. It was the closest. I thought I'd call Fire and Rescue from here."

"Well, do it," I snapped, trying to keep from shaking, "and quit dripping on Carrie's nice carpet. She'll be furious with us both."

Leland blinked twice. "I'm sorry, Sissy," he said, heading for the kitchen.

"I know." I knew he meant sorry about more than the carpet.

"Is Ron around?" he turned hopefully at the door.

I shook my head. "He drove into the city to buy some special surprise for Carrie's birthday. I don't even know how to reach him. He's another one who doesn't believe in cell phones." I ran past Leland back to the kitchen and scooped up Sam and the measuring cups and carried off the whole kit and caboodle so the child wouldn't hear Leland on the telephone. I rocked Sam in the painted white rocker Carrie and I had been rocked in. Knowing Sam, I could see he intended to stay up past midnight, but pretty soon the rocking made him turn loose of his ambition and he drifted off to sleep, leaving me adrift on a river of remembrance.

The memories splashed over me. I had been Cecelia until Carrie was born and then I became Sissy forever after. Not just because Carrie's rosebud mouth couldn't articulate my given name, but because her arrival gave me a new one: I was no longer Cecelia; now I'd become Carrie's Sister, Sissy for short. Even though I came first, once Carrie was on the scene I never came first to mind. I bore the distinction of being both the oldest and an afterthought.

I remembered the time Meema caught Carrie in the barn with a candle. She must have been about five years old when she decided she didn't like facial hair. She wouldn't kiss Dad with his new moustache and she wouldn't even talk to you if you had a beard. Her hatred for facial hair logically included eyebrows. She had tried cutting hers off with a scissors but that hadn't gone very well. So she decided to burn them off. She'd seen Mom and Meema burn pinfeathers off our chickens so she thought it ought to work. And it did. One eyebrow had disappeared by the time Meema found her wailing with the dropped candle smoldering in the straw.

Meema, our soft-spoken, tireless grandmother, screamed and shook her until they were both limp. She demanded to know what Carrie would have done if her hair had caught fire. Three years older than Carrie, I couldn't figure out why nobody screamed or shook her over the chances of the barn catching fire. But I saw it wasn't only other people who got singed in Carrie's presence. I had always known she was a public danger for sure, but I finally realized she was just as dangerous to herself.

When Carrie was older (but still, of course, relentlessly younger than her big sister) just her presence was enough to activate fireworks, "Pyrotechnics," O'Pa would accuse. Even when you stood one on one with Carrie, you'd feel the tingle of sparks flying off her, but as soon as anyone else came along – the incendiary third party – some kind of explosion always followed, an argument or an accident or someone feeling left out. It wasn't Carrie's fault exactly: it was just the way it was. Boys and girls alike, kids and grownups, relatives and strangers – everyone jostled their neighbor out of the way, everyone pressed to get a little bit closer. O'Pa would order me to "never mind" and thunder that virtue was its own reward, but virtue looked like pretty scant treasure compared to what came Carrie's way.

I waded through her more serious boyfriends, starting all the way back with sweet, steadfast Bob Feltz in grade school who asked her to go steady and vowed to marry her when he turned eighteen. I remembered Floyd Buckley in junior high who stole $20 from his mother's purse to buy Carrie a Jean Naté after-bath-set-with-toiletries case. I remembered Ted Carmichael who was the first boy she went all the way with (the inspiration for me to hurry up with John Brahm which led to my hurry-up wedding: John Jr. raises cattle not ten miles from here). I couldn't forget Bill Miller with his Harley and his hair that came down just over his collar and his arms like tree limbs, knotty with muscle.

I envied Carrie many things but none so much as Bill Miller with his mint-condition body and his Hollywood eyelashes. I ached for Bill Miller and there wasn't much my John Sr. could do that didn't seem weak or ordinary by comparison. (There was a time, just a few years past, I think, when John ached for Carrie in the same way, but one or both of them didn't let the bonfire ignite.) If Bill had been my brother-in-law, across the table for every holiday dinner, across the aisle for all the school pageants, I maybe would have done something that everyone would remember and some of us surely regret, but instead he straddled his bike and rode into the sunset, with no one's arms circling his middle, no one's cheek pressed against his back.

He had given Carrie an ultimatum and in return she gave him his riding papers. I dissolved into tears when she told me, equal parts grief and relief. She was surprised by my reaction but not shocked – nothing ever shocks Carrie.

"Why wouldn't you marry him?" I had to know. "Why?"

She looked at me like I had left the front door gaping during a blizzard. "Why would I?"

I pulled myself together. "Not husband material?" I said, trying to sound like one of the magazines we were always reading to make sense of domestic relations.

"More to the point: not father material," Carrie replied. "You can always get rid of a husband."

But Carrie never had to dispose of a husband because she refused to take one on until she was ready to settle down and have a child (stout-hearted, stout-legged Sam). And then Ron miraculously appeared, floating down the river in a beautiful old dugout canoe. Carrie was submerged in the swimming hole at the end of her property, O'Pa's and Meema's old place, when she bobbed up to compliment Ron on his fine vessel.

Carrie and the canoe drifted side by side while they talked easily about nothing much until Ron realized she was peeled naked, and then, as he says, everything just fell into place. Ron spent that night at Carrie's and every night since. Two years after he nearly floated through her life, Carrie and Ron got married. And three days before their first wedding anniversary and one month before Carrie's thirty-eighth birthday, Sam was born.

While Carrie did settle down, she wasn't transformed by marriage and motherhood. If you were to go into town for a buffet dinner at Rose's Cafe on a weekend in summer, you'd likely hear some group of city floaters talking about how they were out on the river, gliding along counting blue herons like out-of-state license plates, when a mermaid rose from the water and waved at them, her long dark hair falling to, but not covering, her bare breasts. She'd wade over to their canoe, chatting about the weather while they groped for words. I wonder if she even owns a bathing suit.

Folks in town, most particularly the women as you might imagine, used to have fits about Carrie swimming nude in daylight. Especially as they knew she'd met a number of the guys she dated that way. Wives still tell their husbands that word better not come back about them being seen fishing off Carrie's place or they'll get their poles bent when they come home. I've always pretended to be ignorant of such goings-on but I was furious with Carrie for making us the big talk of a small town. On top of that I had to worry about Carrie meeting up with some rough type or, worse, a bunch of rough types. Plenty of city people and not a few local boys treat the river like a moving Mardi Gras, drinking their way from the time they put in until they reach their take-out point at the end of the day. A lot of Budweiser floats down the Meramec. Beer and sun can addle even a regular guy's head. But Carrie always says she can handle herself and to this day she has always been right.

Leland has to be wrong. Dead wrong.

The shriek of a siren sliced through my reveries. God, how I hoped someone would tell Ron what had happened before he got home. I throbbed with the need for something useful to do. But holding Sam was useful. And so was remembering that Carrie can outswim fish and how fierce she can get when she needs to.

Fifteen years ago, the U.S. Army Corps of Engineers and a bunch of real estate developers from the city decided it would be a good idea to have a lake within commuting distance. A big lake for big boats and big resorts and big condominium complexes. A big lake that would swallow up all the small farms.

River rats hold a low opinion of stagnant pools, no matter how big they are; we like our water running. We've learned to live with a trickle or a flood – the fickleness, the aliveness of the river. But the Corps and the developers weren't interested in the preservation of the river rat or the family farm or the wetlands habitat, endangered species though they all be. The decree came down, as though the river didn't belong to us, that the dam would be built no matter what the people living on her banks said.

Neighbor turned against neighbor – for giving in too fast, for selling out. Old grievances and new fears set us apart from one another.

Overnight, hand-lettered signs were taped to store windows. Young and wild as she was, and with a reputation for irresponsibility she had truly earned, Carrie came up with the idea to call a town meeting and, to my surprise, more than her kinfolk showed up. All of a sudden the talk was about solidarity, sticking together, but she said that wasn't enough – we couldn't win the war alone – and she was right. We needed lawyers and teachers of agriculture and engineers of our own and billboards and bumper stickers: we needed the city people. The rest of us got up bake sales and catfish fries to raise money while Carrie drove her old Dodge Ram into St. Louis and called on do-gooders and environmental types she'd met while they were floating our river.

Suddenly we were in the midst of a movement, folks who'd never intentionally been in the midst of anything but hayfields or streams, side by side with city people – brewery workers and registered nurses and members of the Junior League – gathering signatures for an initiative petition. It was like a made-for-TV movie. For a little while it was exhilarating, but still we felt the looming power of the dam even before it was built. We couldn't stop it, we were told: Move aside or go under.

The forced buyout of properties was under way. The Corps' surveyors were busy setting their little orange flags, bright, ugly talismans of the deluge to come. The momentum would carry the dam proponents to victory and our poor struggle would sink to the bottom of the new lake like an old box springs or a rusted-out porch glider.

As suddenly as the first town meeting posters had appeared, those orange plastic surveyors' pennants started disappearing. A colonel from the Corps came to one of our meetings and asked us politely to quit pulling up their flags. He said we knew better than to think we could stop the dam – you know he called it "progress" – from coming that way. But by the look on his face it suddenly seemed maybe we could stop it. Anyway, we could slow it down some. Long enough to collect the signatures we needed.

Nobody glanced Carrie's way during that meeting. Nobody said anything much at all about surveyors or flags until after we got our petition on the ballot and the voters rejected the dam. Then everybody trotted out some story about seeing Carrie riding along on her gray with the white stockings, Old Coot she called him, each evening after the surveyors quit work, pulling up the flags they had just reset. "She taught the Corps a thing or two about 'pulling up stakes,'" Jed Taylor would say with his rough, splintery laugh.

So the town sort of forgave Carrie's skinny dipping when they decided she had a special kinship with the river. I remember our high school principal Bea Freivogel saying, just a few years back, that I was my mother's daughter but Carrie belonged to the river, "like Romulus and Remus with the River Tiber, like Moses and the Nile."

Nearly the only criticism you heard about Carrie after that was she'd ruined Old Coot. You couldn't get a decent ride out of him. Until the day he keeled over in the south pasture, no matter who was on his back, that horse would come to a dead halt whenever he hit a spot where the surveyors had planted those flags. He'd lower his front end like a circus pony, patiently waiting for his rider to pull what was only a memory up from the soil.

So what would everybody say now? Smooth round words about how even death couldn't come between Carrie and her river? Maybe there was something fitting in that, something literary, but it felt like a slap in the face.

Ron came home while I was still rocking Sam, back and forth as though as long as we kept moving the river and all its sorrows couldn't reach us. Ron's face was so lit up, I could see he'd found the perfect present for Carrie's fortieth birthday. For one small moment I wondered if she couldn't face the thought of growing older and then I was ashamed of myself. Carrie had been able to face school principals and protective mothers and the Army Corps of Engineers and our O'Pa. Age wouldn't scare her.

And now I was the one who had to face Ron. He had turned out to be good husband and father material. Even a decent brother-in-law. I wished John Sr. would show up and take this burden from me.

But it wasn't John who relieved me of my horrible announcement. Leland came careening through the house until he found us, frozen, me unable to form the words and Ron unable to ask me what terrible thing it was I had to say.

Leland looked like death warmed over. "It was Mary Beth Loomis!" he shouted, waking up Sam. "It wasn't Carrie at all!"

"Are you sure?" I said, tears finally flowing, streams of joy and of sorrow.

"Sure sure," he said firmly. "I came as quick as I could." He shivered in the doorway, from horror or relief or cold or all of them.

Ron looked from one to the other of us. He knew he'd hear it all and that the danger was past so he just let us finish up in our own way.

"But you said dark hair," I reproached Leland. "Mary Beth has red hair." I avoided saying "had."

"Well, I guess it looked dark, being wet and all."

"And the body. Why, Mary Beth's only twenty years old." I would grieve for Mary Beth and the Loomis family later.

"I guess that was a trick of the water too," Leland mumbled.

"More like a trick of memory," I said, flying high now. I couldn't help it – being happy. "Oh, Leland, look at you. Are you trying to set some sort of record by dripping in every room in this house?" I handed Sam over to his father and reached for a clean diaper to mop up with. But first I pressed it to my eyes. I didn't give a hoot where Carrie had gone or what she'd been up to while I'd sat rocking, but I wasn't going to let another day pass without asking what in Lucifer's name she'd done with all those orange flags.

} RELATIVE STRANGERS {

The closer she got to Lake Geneva, the heavier Carla's heart hung in her chest. In times past, the journey had always had the opposite effect. Before, worries and sorrows seemed to recede into the city. Even while Opa was dying, the time spent at her grandfather's bedside wasn't painful. At the lake even the sadness tasted sweet.

As she drove the familiar road, ticking off landmarks – Go-Krazy Go-Kart, the Shell station where Earl's Sunoco used to be, the Cheese Box – Carla parsed the sentence her mother had opened the phone conversation with: "Oma kicked Tante out of the house!" As usual, Oma was the subject, Tante the object, but always before the verb had been passive-aggressive.

"You have to talk to her," her mother had pleaded. "You're the only one she might listen to."

"Me?" Carla was already calculating when her ten o'clock appointment with a consignor would end and how soon she could close the shop. "What can I possibly do?"

"Reason with her. Make her understand how cruel this is," Ursula coached. "Find out if she's gone crazy."

Carla exhaled deeply. "How did you hear about it?" Surely her mother hadn't received any news from Oma's neighbors. "Did Tante call?"

"Your oma did! Before I was even out of bed. She said, 'Ursula, your Tante Emilie is living at the Harbor Shores. I thought you'd want to know.' Just like that. Then she said, 'It's a Best Western.' Like that made everything all right! Do you think she's finally lost it? Maybe your opa's death was more of a shock than we realized." Ursula paused. "Do you think it's Alzheimer's?"

} {

Two weeks before, when the family returned to the house following Opa's funeral, Oma announced she would soon be writing a will. Her husband gone, she had plans of her own. Oma's audience hushed as she launched into her prepared speech. The Lake Geneva property would be bequeathed to one among her nineteen grandchildren. She had decided only one person should hold the title so no others could force a sale. (The thought of a resort or condos or even a half-dozen suburban gothic fortresses replacing the sprawling frame house etched two white, vertical lines on either side of her mouth.) The previous day she had told an ambitious real estate broker who appeared uninvited at her door that her late husband Yannick owned a gun for the sole purpose of shooting verdammt developers and, before he died, he'd insisted she learn how to use it.

She wished it all kept in the family, for the family. "If one person inherits, then whole family will keep," she congratulated herself in her stunted English. None of the family questioned that the children would be passed over in favor of the grandchildren.

One of the grandchildren, who could afford to be generous as he was quite certain not to be the one chosen, suggested she might want instead to will the property to Tante Emilie who was, after all, a dozen years younger than Oma (and more favorably disposed toward him) and could reasonably be expected to live a good long time yet, having the same hearty genes as her older sister. Of course Tante would then will the property to one of them, having no friends and no other living relatives (once Oma died) than her nieces, nephews, grandnieces, and grandnephews.

These startling comments had the effect of turning Oma's soliloquy into a debate, by introducing the notion that her will – not the legal document but her volition – might actually be challenged. The sons and daughters of Oma and Opa, along with their spouses, all hazarded into this uncharted territory, as though their opinions mattered. Kurt, the tire dealer, said he was sure that whoever inherited would let Tante Emilie stay on in the house until she died. Oma said his was a very round idea but with a large hole in the middle. Janet, the kindergarten teacher, said the will could be written so as to give Tante the right to live there throughout her lifetime but grant her no actual control over the property. Oma congratulated Janet on her law degree. "Do you win many cases in the sandbox?" Tante Emilie was in her bedroom during this discussion, not that any of her family had troubled to ascertain her whereabouts.

Fortunately, everyone came to their senses and let the matter rest. The time for argument, if that time ever came, would be much later. This was not the occasion to finally rebel against Oma's dictates.

Her rule had always been law. She and Opa married young but they hadn't been blessed with children for almost a decade, so she had become quite set in her ways before turning her hand to motherhood. By that time, her husband Yannick had already sent for her little sister Emilie, so the children would scurry to their young, pliant aunt when their mother presented too stern a face.

Yet Oma had been the heart of the family. And their whole world growing up had consisted of family, Carla's mother had explained. Ursula's parents didn't socialize. The household was a world unto itself. Her mother and aunt seldom left the three acres of shoreline that comprised their "yard," except to go to Mass on Sundays and Confession once a month. They hardly ever shopped, having their groceries delivered to the house. They didn't even attend meetings of the parish Altar and Rosary Society.

Duties were divided between the sisters. Tante took care of the laundry and the housecleaning, Mutti the gardening and cooking. Yannick built homes for other people around the lake and brought in good money which seldom got spent. Carla's mother hoped that "whoever" inherited the real estate also inherited enough of that cash to keep the property in good repair. The house was a true dowager: old-fashioned but substantial, and in need of constant attention.

Carla was the heir apparent, not just because she was the oldest grandchild and the oldest child of Oma's oldest child, but because she was closest to Oma. She had spent the most time in Oma's company. Ursula had returned to the lake to live with her parents when Carla's father was drafted and sent to Viet Nam right before Carla turned three years old.

As often happens with strict parents, Oma changed course, veering toward indulgence or at least tolerance with the advent of her first grandchild, though this tenderheartedness didn't carry over into her dealings with adult family members. She remained taciturn with her sister, who tried to keep out of her path; gruff with her husband, who shrugged and did whatever he pleased; and critical of her children, who married early and moved far away.

Carla's mother was the exception, returning home for those two years and settling afterward in Chicago, close enough for weekend visits and to send the grandchildren for extended stays. These were true vacations for Carla as at her grandparents' house she was released from having to act as Little Mother to her four younger brothers.

Carla and her brothers spent their summer days on the water, their summer nights in the white frame house. Everyone was expected to play an instrument (Oma didn't permit a television set on the premises). Carla had become the family violinist, mostly to please her grandmother. Opa wheezed on his Hohner harmonica. The two oldest of Carla's brothers wielded guitars, the other two preferred drums, but Oma did not permit drums in the house. (Drums and television headed a long list of things verboten.) So, while at the lake, one of the two younger boys would play the recorder; the other took up the harmonica, perhaps to show solidarity with his grandfather, whose instrument Oma dismissed as suitable only "for boating." Oma and Tante Emilie had both chosen the piano, so they could never perform at the same time.

Many evenings they would entertain one another, sometimes as an ensemble, sometimes taking turns performing solo. On these musical nights, after busy, athletic days, Carla often thought that here, needing no outsiders, was a latter-day version of the von Trapp family, except that Oma discouraged any singing.

} {

For the first time, thoughts of the lake house oppressed her. It was an enormous white albatross slung round her neck. The house demanded year-round occupancy. And then there were the gardens. And the ongoing battle to keep the damp at bay. Oma was forever ordering the windows shut, to prevent white streaks of moisture from blooming on dark, polished wooden surfaces and to keep the piano in tune.

Carla didn't want to leave Chicago and her friends and her shop. *Bizarre/Bazaar* carried furniture and art works on consignment – perfectly nice things that had been supplanted because of a new color scheme or sudden passion for faux animal skins – and antiques and oddments she picked up, sometimes along the route between the city and Lake Geneva.

The shop was doing well, mostly because Carla had a knack for display. She'd pile fresh apples in an open desk drawer or drip a silk piano scarf from a folding wooden screen and customers would be coaxed into giving the pieces a second look. Somehow, in juxtaposition like that, the merchandise didn't seem ordinary. Carla was selling the idea that ownership of something from her store conferred distinction upon the owner.

She wanted to keep the shop, which was located one block from her favorite restaurant, two blocks from her apartment, three blocks from the small theatre group she had recently become involved with, six blocks from Wrigley Field, and worlds away from the white frame house. The lake house had always offered escape; now she wanted to escape from it. Part of her said to relax: nothing had happened yet, nothing that made her responsible; Oma could live for another decade. But the rest of her – her bones and marrow, her soft organs – confirmed that the burden was already hers. Otherwise she wouldn't be driving to see Oma when she should be polishing those brushed-steel serving pieces with the Bakelite handles.

Poor Tante Emilie.

With a jolt Carla realized she had always thought that: Poor Tante Emilie. Emilie had been a girl in her teens when Opa had sent the passage money and she'd been an indentured servant ever since. She'd never had any life apart from the family. Everyone loved Tante – that went without saying – but no one respected her. As far as Carla could tell, not even Tante herself.

The crunch of Carla's tires on the gravel drive brought Oma to the door. She stood with hands clasped at the waist, a stout Bruegel figure. When Carla climbed the steps, her grandmother presented a dry cheek for kissing.

"Mom called this morning," Carla said. She had no idea what to say next.

Oma nodded. "'Telephone, telegram, tell Ursula' – the whole family will be talking by now. It is easier than writing letters to everyone."

"What happened? Why did Tante leave?"

"I told her to get out."

"But why?"

"I will not have a whore living in my house."

"Tante Emilie?" Carla's eyes filled her face. "I can't imagine anyone less deserving of such…such a title."

"Feh. And always I am thinking you have good imagination."

"Oma, she's your sister. Whatever caused this quarrel between you will blow over in a day or two."

"Not in one hundred years."

"Will you tell me?"

"Come inside." Her eyes raked the vast, unoccupied landscape. "The neighbors do not need to know our business."

When they were seated at the kitchen table, Oma said, "You cannot change my mind. And I will not change my mind. That woman is gone from this house. I clean my own house from now on."

"But how can you accuse her of..." she shook her head "...behaving badly when she was closed up in the house all the time? I never saw her go anywhere."

"Where should she go? She was your grandfather's whore." Oma played the disclosure like the trump card it was.

"What?"

"Now your hearing is as no good as your imagination?"

Carla could see that Oma, at least for that moment, was enjoying herself. She was as shocked by the insight as by her grandmother's announcement. "Is this supposed to be a joke?"

"Are you laughing?"

"Not at all. But I think maybe you are."

"Maybe. The last laugh."

"You're saying Opa and Tante had an affair, is that it?"

"No."

"Thank God."

"Affair is something with beginning and end. Your Onkel Karl had affair with his receptionist. It last until your Tante Susan decide to go work for him. That is affair."

"Ugh. I really didn't need to know that."

"Your opa with his whore – that was not affair, that was for always."

Carla puzzled over this. "Did you just find out? When Opa was dying?" She wondered if it had been a deathbed confession, if her grandfather had tried to gain his wife's forgiveness before seeking that of his Creator. Or if Tante had betrayed herself in her grief.

"Do you think your oma is stupid woman? Or blind? I know from first day."

"Then why didn't you put a stop to it?" Carla didn't suppose the timid sister, or the burly husband for that matter, could have defied this woman for very long.

"From first day, what I stop was caring for Yannick or for Emilie. So, I have no husband, no sister. I am alone."

"Why didn't you leave him?"

Oma looked hard at her. "And I go where? For me there is nothing back in Germany. I am old married woman. Who wants me? And I am Catholic. To leave my husband is more sin. So I stay. And God give me reward. He give me four children." Oma gazed out the kitchen window in the direction of the lake.

"You didn't become pregnant until after...after Opa and Emilie...?"

Oma turned her head sharply back to face Carla. "Me? I never become pregnant." She sighed, "I think maybe Yannick not take up with Emilie if I could make babies of my own. Maybe."

Stunned, Carla stared at the grain of the oak beneath her palms. She recalled the times she had stood beside Oma, rolling out tissue-thin sheets of dough on the scrubbed, worn surface. Opa would say their strudel made his heart sing. Or rather, made his heart "zing."

"But then," Carla frowned with the strain of putting the thought into words, "then Tante is my real oma." She wanted to retreat into the darkened living room, with its drapes perpetually drawn to protect the lustrous Bechstein upright, and lie down on the tufted sofa, watched over by the flock of porcelain bird figurines from Germany, and try to digest this revelation. But Oma wasn't going to let the conversation rest there.

"No! I am real! She is not real wife. Not real mutti. Not real oma."

Carla was sure she had gone over this list in her head many times before.

"Not real sister. Only real whore."

"My God, Oma. You've lived together all these years with this between you, and finally Tante is old, too. Why kick her out now?"

"Now it is my house."

While Oma was in the side garden harvesting the first tender blades of lettuce, Carla telephoned her mother in Chicago and told her, trying to sound matter-of-fact, trying to keep the horror from creeping through. Her mother gasped and then was quiet. "Mom?" Carla said.

"I thought it was just Gert," Ursula said apologetically. "It never occurred to me it could have been all of us."

"You knew?"

"Yes. Well, I knew and I didn't know. You know how those things are."

"No. I don't." Carla thought she might never again consider herself to be one who knows how anything is.

"I was six, almost seven when Tante must have been pregnant with Gert. I mean, no one talked about it, but I was old enough to notice she was getting bigger and bigger, as big as women who had babies. Then they told us we had a new baby sister. The boys weren't old enough to ask questions. And I was just old enough to know better than to ask questions. So, I put it out of my mind."

"That was it? You just put it out of your mind?"

Ursula spoke haltingly: "Sometimes I felt sorry for Gertie, because maybe Mutti wasn't her real mother. Sometimes I'd feel sorry for Mutti having an extra child to take care of." She paused, considering. "I never felt sorry for Tante though, for having her baby taken away. If what I suspected was true, then I thought she'd been lucky, not being sent to a home for unwed mothers, or just sent away, but kept safe in Mutti's house, safe from the shame of it and from the responsibilities. Safe. That's a good one, isn't it?" Ursula's voice caught. "I didn't know your grandfather was part of the equation."

Carla hesitated, then asked, "You really never said anything?"

"No. Not to anyone."

"Not to Dad?"

"No. He had a hard enough time getting used to my family as it was."

"Not even to Aunt Gert?"

"She was the last person I'd tell! What if I was wrong? Worse still, what if I was right? And I didn't want to hurt Tante Emilie who was always so sweet to us. Besides, if it wasn't true, then there was something wrong with me for inventing it. If it was true, then there was something wrong with my family. Which meant there was something wrong with me."

"How old do you think she was? Tante Emilie, I mean. When Opa…?"

"If she's my mother – oh, dear God, she *is* my mother, she is *my* mother – she would have been – Lord! – fifteen when I was born."

Carla sucked in her breath. "Your father was a bastard."

"No," her mother laughed weakly, "but all his children are."

"Poor Tante Emilie."

"God, yes," her mother concurred.

Carla ran up the stairs to the Girls' Room, the sunnier of two large bedrooms outfitted like a dormitory for visiting grandchildren, and grabbed one of the dozen cast-off swimsuits layered in the bottom drawer of the curvaceous mahogany dresser with its freckled mirror. She scanned her reflection, looking for traces of Tante Emilie. Turning away from the glass, she had one clear objective: to dive into the cold, deep lake.

As she crossed the lawn, she could see them distinctly, each moving in a different sphere, unconnected to the others: Oma in her eternal, navy-blue skirted swimsuit, her powerful arms and legs churning the surface of the lake; Opa mowing the lawn in his uniform of Dickies and a plaid shirt, or peeled down to a sleeveless undershirt; Tante in her "wrappers," cotton housedresses whipped by the wind from the lake as she methodically loaded or stripped the clothesline. Tante remained fearful of the water and the predators lurking just below the smooth, glassy skin. Freshwater or no, she sensed creatures with long, tentacled arms or large skatelike wings waiting to embrace her. Tante had once asked Carla her opinion on the existence of carnivorous seaweed.

The water shocked her body. She thought for a moment about swimming far enough from shore so she wouldn't be able to get back before the cold overpowered her, numbed her thoughts and her limbs. If she drowned, Oma would see how destructive the exile of Tante was to the family. Carla hauled herself up onto the dock, arms and legs blue and trembling, cheeks ruddy with embarrassment. She sputtered to unseen, unmet neighbors, "You people have no idea what you've been missing."

She toweled off and dressed hurriedly, leaving the wet suit dripping in the upstairs bathroom and a note for Oma on the dresser, saying only that she'd phone tomorrow. She rushed past other bedrooms, not pausing to calculate who had actually slept where. Slipping out by the seldom-used front door, she avoided the old woman rattling pots in the kitchen and drove to the Harbor Shores, showing up, unannounced, at Tante Emilie's room.

}{

On the ride over, Carla had erased her picture of the woman she'd believed her great-aunt. Either Tante would be transformed from her pallid self by her new independence, however unwelcome it might be, or Carla would now see her differently. Whatever she was, she was not the colorless spinster they all – except perhaps Carla's mother (and of course Oma) – had imagined her to be. This Emilie had been somebody's lover. She had borne four children.

When Emilie opened the door, she looked disappointingly like herself, perhaps more so. In addition to the general almost-ness of her (the almost-white of her hair, the almost-blue of her eyes, the almost-grace of her figure), she had a distracted air. A swell of pity washed over Carla for poor, poor Tante Emilie.

"Oh, Tante," she said, kissing the damp cheek, and the pale eyes flooded.

"She told you," Emilie said flatly, blotting her face on a hand towel with a large blue HS stamped above the hem.

"Yes."

"It's not fair."

"I know. It was all so long ago. You were just a child really." Carla felt that Oma, though wronged, would have done better by the family by burying the secret with her husband.

"All those years I wanted to tell and she wouldn't let me."

This startled Carla.

"She stole everything from me. Not just my babies. Everything."

"But, Tante" – should she call her Oma now? maybe Tante Oma? – "you must understand how angry and hurt she had been for all those years."

"She angry? She hurt? Why? Everything happened as she wanted. She couldn't make babies, so she told Yannick to send for me. Then she sent him to my bed. I didn't want him there. She got what she wanted and still I had to have him on top of me, crushing me, because she wouldn't let him touch her any more. Even when he was dying and I was cleaning him," she shuddered, "that old man put his big hands on me. And she didn't even love the children. She just kept them like she keeps china birds in the living room. It was only the grandchildren she could love. My grandchildren."

"You mean that Oma approved?" Carla said, as though Emilie's speech hadn't been crystalline in its clarity.

Emilie snorted, "Approved! It was her idea. Even if Yannick had ever thought of it, he would have been too afraid of her to try."

"Monsters," Carla said wonderingly, trying out the word aloud.

"Monsters," Tante Emilie affirmed with some satisfaction.

They talked for nearly two hours, Emilie reciting a gothic tale of home births with her sister in attendance as midwife. "When my milk came in, hard, she never let me have my babies. It was Yannick who sucked me." The one revelation Carla refused, repelled by this stranger itching to unveil the most delicate intimacies, was the explanation of how Emilie managed to stop bearing children.

Carla ordered room service for Emilie, who couldn't remember when she had last eaten. After setting her up at the little desk overlooking the lake with a cup of soup and a half-sandwich from room service, Carla went down to the lobby to again phone her mother. She gave Tante's side of the story.

"Do you believe her?" Carla's mother couldn't help asking.

"She's not lying, if that's what you mean. But Oma was telling the truth, too."

They were both silent, then Carla said, "I'm glad Opa is dead. Aside from him raping his jailbait sister-in-law, I don't think I could stand a third version of the family history." She didn't stop to think how any of these words might affect her mother, his daughter.

"What are you going to do next?" Ursula shifted abruptly.

"Gather up her stuff, which shouldn't take long – I don't think she's unpacked her suitcase – and take her back to the city. Unless you have a better suggestion."

"No. She certainly can't stay where she is."

"I only have the one bedroom."

"You'll bring her here. I've already changed the sheets in your old room."

"What did Dad say?"

"Well, he's pretty much in shock, like the rest of us. I thought he might bring up nursing homes, but he just said, 'We'll see if this new mother of yours is any easier to get along with than the old one.'"

} {

Almost as soon as her seatbelt was fastened, Tante Emilie fell asleep in the passenger seat, her head dipping and bobbing like a buoy. Carla was grateful for the silence and drove as smoothly as she could to preserve it, avoiding sharp turns or depressions in the pavement.

Had the neighbors known? Is that why the family had been left to themselves? And the priest? What had the sisters whispered in their confessions?

The most hateful part was having to revise her memories. Nothing had been as it appeared: all false fronts. The inculcation of straitlaced traditions and old-world values – the overweening togetherness – now seemed a sinister deception. The two-story house, with the broad, window-filled addition Opa had built facing the lake, was only a façade, a stage-set for the perverted version of the Trapp Family players.

But then, she thought, she and her mother – all the jumble of children and grandchildren – were not the only casualties. Both Oma and Tante were victims, probably Opa too. So much longing. Physical longing, a longing for status, for heirs. A fretwork of loneliness propped up the white house. Such a legacy. Suddenly it struck Carla how no one was suggesting the secret be perpetuated. Her mother had broadcast the news – as Oma had foreseen – not sensationally, but resolutely. Ursula had taken on the burdens of setting the record straight and of welcoming Emilie into her home, preserving the connections she'd been brought up to value.

Carla decided then that she would keep the house, keep it in the family and for the family. She would manage, even if it meant asking subscriptions from the various cousins and uncles and aunts to cover expenses. When the house became hers, the first thing she would do was open every window, welcoming the breeze off the lake.

} SORTING {

She was bent over the heap of dirty clothes, sorting them into three piles according to commercial prescription. All the permanent press, forever new materials, there. The darks, Jane's tights, and her own Indian cotton shirts there. The whites and Emily's grass-stained wheat jeans there. It was a sort of alchemy, this compounding of detergent and pre-soak powder, bleach and borax and fabric softener. When the clothes came out of the enameled white cauldron, all trace of bodies would be purged from them. Creases at the elbow, wrinkled backs, smells of tobacco, bottled scent, and musky sweat, the noose of oil around the collars and the bracelet of dirt at the cuffs would be removed. The clothes would be fresh and hopeful, beckoning from drawers and closets.

She didn't hear the footfall on the steps over the complaint of the washing machine. She didn't sense another presence. So she was both startled and afraid when Jane appeared deus ex machina before her. She remembered her own childhood instructions to call out continually as she descended to the dank labyrinth of the basement. If she failed to signal her arrival, she would be met by her mother's angry "You frightened me" instead of "How was school?" There was something about basements that made you expect an intruder to find you there.

"Hi, Mom. What's for snack?"

She remembered how foolish and alone she had felt as she had voiced her tentative hello on each step. She bit off her outpouring of fear, swallowing it, and said, "Hi, honey. There's apple juice and a loaf of zucchini bread."

Jane was halfway to the kitchen when she called back, "I love bikini bread."

The girl returned to the laundry room carrying her cup of juice and a paper napkin with a rough-hewn slice of the bread upon it. She set these down on the unsteady metal TV table and settled herself onto the maple kitchen chair that had been parted from its back some years ago and relegated to the basement. Her legs dangled above the streaked concrete floor and she looked small even for her six years.

"How was school?"

"Okay."

"What did you learn today?" She tried to remember the formula, her mother's next question.

"Nothing. We had to write a sentence and we had to make it up and I was the only one who put a period."

"Good for you."

"And minuses. I hate minuses. So does Maria. Maria's my best friend."

"I thought Laura was your best friend."

"She is. She's one of my best friends."

"That's nice."

"And Mrs. O'Connor taught us a song." She cleared her mouth of the zucchini bread and sang, "Sweet drummer boy, will you give me your flower? Sweet drummer boy, will you give me your flower? Rat-tat-rat-tatat boom – will you give me your flow-ow-er?"

She had a pretty voice, clear and confident. She was the only one in the family who sang true and effortlessly. When she was a bit older, her ability to carry a tune would be one of the pieces of evidence she would use to bolster her conviction that she was a foundling, not of the same flesh.

"I like that. Sing the rest."

"I forget."

Jane was kicking the rung of the chair, arythmically.

Stop it, she wanted to say, but she knew that the words wouldn't be said but screamed. Sounds bothered her now, tapping sounds, swallowing sounds. A cough in the night would wake her and the fretting maternal instinct to ease it had somehow evaporated, leaving as a relic the bare fretful urge to stifle it. Bad posture irritated her as did school papers left on the dining room table or a jacket thrown across a chair. She heard and saw things she had never noticed before; they commanded her attention now.

"I have a new boyfriend."

For a while yet the boyfriends would retain equal status, as with the limitless crop of best friends, but it wouldn't be long before the announcement was made with some anguish, and then not long after that when such things were no longer announced at all. Emily was only ten and already she had cried herself to sleep because she was so ugly, because she didn't have blonde hair, because she had freckles and a fat nose, because some nameless boy preferred a blonde, clear-skinned, patrician-nosed beauty. And Emily was a beautiful child. But that hardly mattered because she did not know it because he did not know it.

"Oh? Who?"

"Guess."

"Richard."

"No. He's not new."

"Oh." She rummaged in the dusty corners of memory, casting about for a name as the foot ticked away against wood. "Ben," she produced.

"Mom," stretched into two syllables by outrage, "Ben is a brat. He pushes all the time and he doesn't know anything and Mrs. O'Connor said he might have to stay in first grade next year."

"Who then?" She checked the impulse to counsel compassion for the unfortunate Ben who perhaps pushed to make contact, who probably had no best friends.

"Ryan. We changed desks today and he picked the one next to me. He gave me his fat blue pencil with Snoopy on it. And Mrs. O'Connor said we're the best readers in the class."

Made for each other. Sanctioned by authority. She saw in their jointly held best readership the unmistakable pull toward someone of whom it would be said, "He's perfect for her. A charming couple."

"I thought Emily was going to come home before Girl Scouts to get her cookie money."

"She said she'd take it next week."

She thought of herself again, the girl she had been. She had spent one uncomfortable year in scouting, in the unnatural camaraderie of rolled bandages and roundelays. She would sooner have missed a troop meeting than not meet a deadline, stand empty-handed before her leader. She had been a responsible child – her teachers had praised her and her parents had trusted her. Then she became a responsible wife and mother, volunteering her time in the schools and with a teletype service for the deaf, making Swedish rye bread and hand-sewn quilts, not wanting to stand empty-handed.

Her own daughters had to be reminded – no, nagged – to hang up their clothes, finish their homework, practice the piano, return books to the library. She felt responsible for them though she knew that by assuming their responsibility she was stealing from them. But she wanted them to remain children. Not forever, just long enough.

"Mom, do you remember last summer?"

"Yes," she said as she searched about for something to do with her hands, which were working now with no object.

"Do you remember before Daddy left?"

"Yes." She remembered the hot endless days, the steamy dinners with no crisp masculine presence, the sluggish bewilderment that grew finally into searing anger. She remembered the confrontation, she white-hot, he cool as a reproach, her rage so tempered by his frost as to turn to grief. Did he love her, she had asked. He was in love with someone else, he had answered. Such a tired story.

"Do you remember the day Daddy took me and Emily swimming with Linda?"

"Yes." She was removing things from the dryer now, buttoning shirts around hangers, folding, smoothing. That had been a month before he had left, a month before she had asked him. He knew she had been too busy to go with them but she would have invented something to keep her from that outing anyway. She had never liked Linda though she thought her children were nice enough. She felt the injustice of having Linda's children to consider now as well.

"When Daddy and Linda were in the water, they were kissing and stuff. Me and Emily saw them. I guess Daddy loved Linda then instead of you." Jane waited, almost disinterested, for the reaction.

"I guess so." She made her voice flat, even-seamed, like the pants she laid over the hanger. Being the last to know had suddenly taken on new meaning.

She tried to recall Emily's behavior that last month before he left. There had been a problem – an intensive period of disrespect, talking back to adults, "smart-mouthing," as they titled it within the family.

She knew that for Jane that exchange between her father and Linda had only recently, perhaps just as she sat in the basement room, assumed any significance, appeared rabbit-in-the-hat fashion within a context. But Emily had understood, hating her father for his desire, hating her mother because she had lost his desire, hating herself because she loved them both.

She sorted the socks, always last, clinging like parasites to the slick drum of the dryer. For a time she had wanted him back, but that had passed. Then he had wanted to come back; she hoped that had passed as well. Now she simply wanted to feel no more anguish, not her own nor his.

But there was always something, some breach forced in her careful wall of quietude. A disclosure like Jane's that drove her unwillingly to restructure the past. A gesture of Emily's that marked her as her father's daughter, an unbroken link. A collision with an old acquaintance unaware of the reshuffling of households, surnames.

And now this, she laughed.

"What's so funny?"

"This sock."

"That's Daddy's."

"I know." She laughed again, thinking of the mileage that newspaper humorists and standup comedians had wrung out of the unmatched sock, the disappearing act which takes place somewhere between the washer and the dryer, the drawers filled with unpaired crew socks, lonesome argyles. She had laughed at the nonsense because her husband, too, had his collection of one-of-a-kind socks, heel and toe intact but unmated. She saw with a brilliant clarity the sporadic, unpredictable rendering up by the dryer which would henceforth, at odd intervals, yield one of those socks long ago written off as missing in action: it was marriage that made them disappear. "You'll have to start taking them to him," she said.

} S E C O N D   L O V E R {

When my husband walked out and left me with two distraught kids, a crumbling turn-of-the-last-century house, and an empty bank account, I wished for many things. I wished he and his inamorata would, arm in arm, fall down an open manhole, resulting in multiple fractures in three or four legs between them. I wished I would win the Publishers Clearing House Sweepstakes. I wished I could get somebody to live on my horrible third floor and pay me some rent.

We lived only a few blocks from the university and several of our Parkview neighbors had installed graduate students in their empty nooks and crannies. Some had taken in students in exchange for rent money, others for household help. One couple was receiving monthly rent and *au pair* services for their toddler. Of course they did have a renovated carriage house to offer, but their previous grad student had painstakingly restored it. I wanted to get me some of that indentured slavery – or, at the very least, a little extra cash. So I called the university housing office and they sent me some forms. I filled them out but nothing happened. Students drifted into town for the fall semester. Apartment vacancy signs disappeared as though a sign fetishist was stalking the neighborhood. The sidewalks became cluttered with autumn-gilded dead leaves and summer-bronzed young bodies. But nothing happened to me.

I felt disheartened. No, I felt like guano. Rejected by my husband for a dental hygienist who was two years *older* than I was. Rejected sight unseen by every single grad student at the university. Surely there had been some mistake, some filing error in the housing office. I thought my application revealed stupefying tolerance: I would take any nationality, any religion, any sex with any sexual preference. My only suggestion was that they should not be appalled by children and my only caveat was that I preferred that there wouldn't be lots of noise lots of the time. I had listed my occupation as writer so this graduate student should know that s/he was coming to a house where brain waves thrived. No one came. No one even called.

I set about doing what I often do when I feel helpless over something. I wrote about it. I take a kernel of the real thing and I slap fiction all around it and this way I gain some kind of control over whatever is eating at me. I know this isn't how all writers operate. It isn't even how I operate all the time, but it is therapeutic and some-times effective as well.

When I finished "Foreign Exchange" I showed it to my best friend Colin who is also a writer, a poet from Liverpool who teaches in the English department at Washington University. His verdict was, "It's not so much a short story as an exercise in wishful thinking."

That stung. Not the wishful thinking part but the bit about it being not so much a short story.

"The way I see it," he went on heedlessly, "is that you're ready for some kind of relationship but you're still afraid to trust."

"Pul-lease," I said, feeling vastly superior, sulking no more. "Are you transfixed by American daytime television? Reading books like *Women Who Run With the Wolves So They'll Stop Feeling Like Dogs*? My God, you sound like a talk show host."

"We were talking about you."

"*We* were not."

"I'd say you want a man in your life – don't we all? – but you just aren't ready to deal with all the *Sturm und Drang* that goes along with investment in the three Cs: caring, communication, and commitment."

"This is a whole new side to you, Colin, not your best one I'm afraid."

"This is not about me. What is the perfect solution to your particular dilemma? A mythological grad student who rents a room in your house and a small niche in your heart. Someone who's not on equal footing. Someone who, by definition, will be moving on. A limited partnership for a limited time only."

"Maybe I'm on to something. Maybe you should try to get one too."

"Ah, but I'm sure there's only a limited number available."

"Maybe we could share."

"Very kind of you, but I think not. I've always deplored your taste in men."

So there I was on an unseasonably warm afternoon, several weeks into the semester, several months into feeling sorry for myself, sitting on my charming, crumbling tiled front porch reading Doris Lessing's *Summer Before The Dark* and thinking about coloring the emerging gray in my hair, when a head appeared above the top of my tentacled spirea bushes. He looked something like a lion, his large head fringed round by a tawny mane. "Oh!" I said, startled by this invasion of my property, if not my privacy. "What do you want?" I added ungraciously, once more acutely aware there was no man about to call upon for protection. "Well?" I said, standing to show I was a no-nonsense type, someone to be reckoned with.

"Excuse me," he said. "Is this the house of Frau Voolf?" He was squinting at an index card snugly bracketed in his big palm.

"Wolff?" I said. "Yes. Yes, it is."

"I am come," he said.

"Good for you," I said. He frowned. "Look, I'm sorry but I think you're looking for some other Wolff Frau. I'm not expecting anyone."

He handed me up the index card through the tops of the bushes. There it was: my name and address and a sum of money to be paid monthly – black type on white card, incontestable.

"You have already somevun living on your third floor?" he asked sadly.

"Well, no," I said with some reluctance now that I was face to face with the prospect. "You're from Wash U? But classes started weeks ago."

"Yah, vell, I come here vith my girlfriend and ve are living together by the Loop in vun apartment for two people but ve are having a fight and she is going back to Chermany and I cannot stay any more in this apartment for so much money." He shrugged.

All my imperiousness and irony melted away. I knew what it was like to be impoverished and abandoned. I came down the steps and thrust out my hand. "My name is Annie Wolff," I said. "You'll have to call me Annie. No one ever calls me 'Frau,' not even in English."

And so arrived Hubert, or Hoo-bairt, as he and therefore we pronounced it. He was a model boarder. He paid his rent promptly. He agreed to rake leaves/shovel snow/mow grass according to the season and in return I agreed to edit his philosophy papers and correct his spoken English. He cleaned up the kitchen as soon as he finished eating. He never left his clothes to ferment in the washer. He didn't own a radio or CD player or anything that made noise and he only played mine when I was out. He always knocked politely – even on open doors – so as not to startle us with his presence. He would occasionally ask to join us if the kids and I were watching something on television. He even seemed to like my kids, but not enough to make him suspect. He never complained about the peeling wallpaper and cracked plaster on the third floor or having to share the bathroom on the second floor with the three of us. And he never entertained, even though I encouraged him to.

"You *live* here, you know," I would say brightly. "Invite your friends over. Just give me some warning if you're going to have a party or something so the kids and I can be elsewhere or rent movies and be invisible."

"Yah sure," he would say. "I don't know so many friends here yet that you should be inwisible."

"Well, feel free," I would say vaguely.

"Yah, sure. Thank you wery much."

I didn't ask him to join family dinners with us but I had taken to inviting him to dessert whenever I had friends over for dinner. I felt that a dessert invitation was hospitable enough yet still allowed me to maintain my distance. I didn't want him to feel snubbed, but I did want him to find his own circle of friends among his peers.

One night following a dessert of raisin-coconut bread pudding with rum sauce, Hubert was helping me clear the table after the guests had left. Our hands reached for the sauce bowl at the same moment and then his hand closed over mine. He gave me a gentle tug and spun me into his embrace, my back snugly fitted against his chest. "This is not a good idea," I said. Suddenly every part of my body was remembering just how long it had been since I'd been this close to flesh I wasn't mother to. I could feel his breath on my hair. "Hoo boy," I gasped.

"Hoo-bairt," he corrected. "It is the best idea."

"No," I said firmly. "It would make everything so...so difficult." I sounded resolute but his hot breath was daunting. I had to extricate myself before he happened upon the back of my neck. "You live here," I said as stiffly as I could manage.

"That is vhy it vill be so easy," he said, holding me tighter. "Ve are living here together." Then it happened: he began to nuzzle the nape of my neck. The eternally cold stone that I carried in the pit of my stomach instantly dissolved from the heat coursing through me from the hot spot at the back of my neck. Like a kidney stone zapped by a laser. I was his. For the night. Well, for a portion of it.

We had an arrangement. There were to be no public displays of affection, no proprietary airs, nothing to give us away to children or neighbors, friends or foes. We would meet discreetly on the third floor for periodic releases of sexual tension. The way I saw it we were both lonely and we weren't harming anyone, just helping each other get through a difficult period. Hubert agreed readily to all my stipulations and abided by them. I think, for both of us, the coolness of our social commerce lent a degree of heat to our private commerce.

He was a refreshingly eager – the word robust comes to mind – if not wholly satisfying lover, and his compliments were more than generous. "No Cherman girls know to do these things that you do," he would say as I dressed to return to my downstairs life.

"I'm sure German women do," I would pat his hand, slightly annoyed. Feeling more like an experienced madam than one man's Frau for the past ten years, I would steal down to my own bedroom, which, by unspoken compact, he was not to enter. I never slept beside him, not even on those nights when the kids stayed at their father's.

We perked along, clumsy and yet comfortable – we were comically polite to one another – with what we called our "tutoring sessions" until one night Colin came over for dinner.

Colin was shooting off little barbs here and there. He was in a snit about something his department chair had said to him and was determined that the whole world should feel equally prickly. I was feeling sated and self-satisfied so his needling wasn't getting under my skin, but then Hubert came downstairs to join us for dessert.

"Here, my good man," Colin rose to his feet, acting out some cocktail scene from an old movie, "by all rights you should have my chair, head of the table and all that."

"Pip, pip, Colin. Cheerio," I said warningly. Colin, the stinker, was the only one who knew of our arrangement and had been immensely but quietly amused these last weeks. He gave Hubert an enormous wink and shifted to an empty chair.

"Thank you," said Hubert, clearly puzzled but probably assuming he had lost something in translation. "You are wery kind."

"An American trait, wouldn't you say, old chap? Must be something I've picked up over here. Always willing to share. Especially the women. Quite noble when you think of it."

"Oh, shut up, Colin," I said.

He ignored me and gave Hubert his full attention. "It's an interesting case of the American spirit of generosity and the German willingness to experiment. Very cutting edge of you, Hubert."

"Vhat is?" Hubert said, jumping headlong into Colin's snare.

"To be made use of so unconventionally and then to find oneself made use of as a literary convention as well."

"A literary conwention? I am sorry. I do not understand," Hubert said.

"*I* am sorry. Colin is being a jerk," I said. "A complete *schweinhundt*, who is just now going home."

"Without dessert?" Colin said, looking longingly at his mounded plate.

"Goodnight, Colin."

Colin departed and I resumed my place at the table opposite Hubert. He was looking at me expectantly. "Wait a minute," I sighed and stood up. I came back to the dining room with the story in hand. "Colin thought he was being funny. He was referring to this. 'Foreign Exchange.' It's a story I wrote. Almost a month before you moved in. You'd better read it." I cleared away Colin's dishes from in front of him and set the manuscript down in their place.

When he finished the story, he kept his eyes on the last sheet. Hubert's large leonine head hung over the dining room table, his paws no longer turning pages but now outstretched, sphynxlike, on either side of the stack of papers. His forehead was so furrowed and buckled that I wanted to inspect his fists for a thorn.

"This is wery strange," he said.

"Don't I know it," I said, rolling my eyes. "Imagine how I felt when you showed up in my yard and you were a *German*. I mean you could have been from Nigeria or Scotland, but you weren't. You could have been a female, but nope. It was as though you were following my script. Not that I planned to follow it any further. You do know that, don't you? I mean I was resolved not to even *think* about messing around with you, and I didn't. Really. Until that night. For me it wasn't even a possibility. But maybe deciding that something isn't a possibility makes it possible after all. I mean in order to rule something out, you first have to bring it into the realm of possibilities, don't you?"

Hubert was looking up at me now, rather intently.

"Hey, you can't think it's any stranger than I do," I said. "You know, there is something, well, metaphysical about words set on paper."

"I did not know you vere such a rich voman," Hubert blinked.

"Me? I'm not. Oh. You're talking about *her*." I rolled my eyes again. "Look, Hubert, I know the language thing makes this even more complicated than it would be anyway, but you have to understand that this is fiction.

"Just because a writer uses something real, people think that it's all real, that she – he didn't invent anything." I snapped my fingers in the air to make something, some comprehension, magically appear. "People think you're just a court reporter and you don't get any credit. And then they think that they suddenly *know* you."

"I don't get any credit?"

"Not you. Me. Sometimes when I've written something that sprang from something real," I said, suddenly eager, remembering that this was a student of philosophy I had cornered here, "when it's finished, when it has set a while and I go back to it, I can't tell any more where the real leaves off. And the longer it sets, the more blurred the line becomes."

I sighed profoundly, took a breath, and continued, "About two years ago Colin said something, well, unkind to me. I was really hurt by it. So I made a character out of him and put him into a story and had him behave very much worse than he had that night. I had him say *terrible* things. Later I let Colin read the story. I was a wreck while he read it. I thought the story worked pretty well but I was afraid he'd be furious with me. Instead he *apologized* for all those terrible things he hadn't said." I lifted my shoulders, still surprised by the memory. "I had created

Colin's past. You see? He accepted himself as I had written him. And he's a writer, for Christ's sake. He of all people should have known better. But I guess writers are just as willing as anybody else, maybe more so, to let a writer play God."

Hubert was looking into my eyes now. It was clear he had considered what I'd been saying and had finally come to some conclusions he was ready to reveal. I prepared myself to be enlightened by my philosophy graduate student.

"I do not vant to be a playball for your writing!" the lion roared.

"Hubert, I wrote that before you came to live here," I reminded him primly.

"Maybe."

"And it was your idea that we go to bed together in the first place."

"If you wrote this before I come to live here, then it vas your idea in the first place," he said, making me think of a fox and a block of wood at the same time. "If Colin had not been a jerk tonight, vould you have showed to me this?" He studied my face.

"I don't know." He was taking every word I said and translating it. Who knows how I was coming across in German? "Probably not."

"I vill go to my room and vork now."

"But you haven't had your dessert. Nobody's had any dessert."

} {

After a day of pouting, Hubert asked if I had any time "awailable" for tutoring so we resumed our sessions.

One morning, after the kids were safely in school, I was lying beside Hubert, daydreaming. He was tracing little circles on my breast, a habit of his after making love. "There is chust vun thing I vant to know," he said softly. "Who is this Verner?"

"Hoo boy, Hubert! Yiminy Cricket! There is no Werner. There never was any Werner!"

"Then I am Verner." He smiled to himself so broadly that I expected him to thump his chest with his free hand.

There isn't even a family resemblance, I thought to myself.

A few days later he asked offhandedly, "How many years you have been in this therapy?"

"I've never been in therapy. Not that I don't need it. Not that I am not thinking about getting some very soon."

"I think you should talk vith your therapist. It seems to me that this is vhat they call denial."

"Look," I said, trying to sound patient, feeling like Jane Goodall chatting with a different species, "that was *Elaine* who was in therapy. Maybe that's hard to believe because I had her say the thing about the skunk and the skank when she was talking about her husband and his girlfriend which *is* something *I* would say. Colin told me to cut that line out, that she never would have said that."

Hubert eyed me strangely but he didn't say anything more then.

Another time he asked me about the two men I had sex with, after my husband and before him.

"What two men?"

"I do not care so much about the first man, but I am vondering if I have ever sometime met the second vun at dessert."

"The second man at dessert?"

"The vun you vere so sexy vith, the vun who vanted to go to church vith you."

"There were no other lovers, Hubert. Pay attention now: I made those up. Everything in 'Foreign Exchange' is fiction. *Fiction.* Get it?"

"Yah, sure," he said. "I get it all right. If you don't vant to talk about this lover, no vun can make you. It is your business."

"And what about my other son, Hubert?" I screeched. "Don't you ever wonder what the hell I've done with him?"

While the formality, the distance between us, had rapidly diminished since he'd read the story, the gulf between us was now a chasm. One of those little paradoxes.

"Vhen I stood up this morning –" he began one evening as I was gathering my clothes from the floor of his bedroom.

"'When I got up,'" I amended.

"Vhen I got up, I vas thinking of how your Verner slept in her room but you never sleep in this room and I never sleep in your room."

"But that's what we agreed to at the very beginning," I said, feeling a little panicky as I pulled on my jeans. "We made rules."

"You made rules. You think because you play God vith your writing you can play God vith my liver."

"I think you mean 'life,'" I stifled a snort.

"And that's another thing. Everyvun outside you – "

"Everyone *other* than you."

"Everyvun other than you is alvays telling me I am speaking wery good English. Only you is telling me – "

"*Are* telling me."

"That my English are – "

"*Is.*"

"Alvays wrong. You vould never talk this vay to Verner," he muttered, barely audible.

"That's not fair, Hubert. You do speak very good English, but you asked me to correct you when you made mistakes. You said you wanted to improve."

"Everyvun outside you think – "

"*Other than* you *thinks*," I said gently.

"That I *have* improved!" he bellowed. "And you know vhat? I think I only make so many mistakes now vhen you are in the room. Vhat do you say to that?"

"I say that it's obvious that the way for you to avoid mistakes is for me to stay out of the room." I stomped downstairs, my shirt still unbuttoned, my shoes dangling from my hand. "Vell, vell, vell," I sneered to myself behind my closed door, "that's the end of that chapter."

Hubert came to me a few days later and suggested that we had both been too hasty, that we should not let a momentary "explosive" destroy what we had between us. I said that it was really better this way, that I realized now that our "tutoring sessions" had left him feeling bad about himself and prevented him from forming any real attachments. He was free, I said.

For the remainder of that semester, Hubert did not exercise his freedom. Instead he took to presenting himself in some state of undress whenever the kids were not around. After he would shower he'd appear in an open doorway with only a towel girding his loins. I had once told him that I found freshly bathed flesh to be nearly irresistible. On mornings when the kids had stayed at their father's he would arrive in the kitchen wearing only his tiny European underpants in primary colors. "It is a fine morning," he would say as though decked out in a three piece suit and bowler hat. "As soon as I stood up this morning I knew the day vould be fine."

Every morning Hubert fixed for himself the same breakfast without variation: a container of plain yogurt mixed with a cup of dry muesli with a banana sliced over the top, two pieces of toast with butter and jam and a large mug of hot milk. He always used exactly the same dishes each morning: the same small serving bowl for his breakfast sludge, the same handpainted dessert plate for his toast, the same big Christmas mug with the fastidiously coifed Santa Claus on it. I had once thought the sameness of his breakfast endearing, the ritual of the dishes sweet. I now found the repetitiveness maddening. I would look away as he spooned the thick, yogurted muesli and imagine him shoveling cement into his mouth. I wanted, I *yearned* to smash my son's Santa-face mug with its marcelled beard and symmetrical spiraling locks.

The more Hubert posed, the easier I found it to embrace celibacy. I recognized that I had depersonalized Hubert – I was even grateful to Colin for he had recognized it first – and turned him into a character. And now, somehow, he had become a caricature.

Finally he stopped. But it was too late. I already loathed him.

Colin came by a couple of weeks into my loathing. He was sympathetic: he had once witnessed Hubert eating breakfast. I told him that Hubert had been deaf to my suggestion that he might find more suitable housing elsewhere. Colin said, "It's simple enough. Just tell your grad stud to pack his bags. After all, it's your house. It's not like he has a lease. Give him two weeks notice if you're feeling bountiful."

"I can't do that. I'd feel guilty," I looked at Colin pitifully. "I can't chuck him out" – I was hoping to persuade him by aping his own patterns of speech – "after having slept with him."

"But there'd be no reason to chuck him out if you hadn't slept with him," Colin said impatiently.

"You see, if we'd been equals and I'd slept with him, then I could tell him to get out. But it wasn't a partnership." I appealed to his native sense of fair play, "It wouldn't be cricket. It would be like sacking the underparlormaid once the earl had his way with her."

"I see," said Colin, seeing my irritating scrupulousness. "Well then, Annie, you'll simply have to endure his breakfasts and his underwear. That's what nobility does. It endures."

About midway through second semester Hubert began entertaining – one young female after another, until he finally settled on a fraulein from Munich who was here as an exchange student at University City High School. I never learned how they met. She had just turned seventeen and Hubert was twenty-four.

"When you said German *girls* didn't know how to...do the things I... used to do," I managed to say icily despite my embarrassment, "I see now that you meant girls."

"I think you are maybe jealous now that I got a girlfriend and you vish you vere not so quick to say 'Bye-bye, Hubert.'"

"On the contrary. I just think she's awfully young for you."

"She is less young for me than I vas young for you."

"Whatever you say," I shrugged. "And however you say it." I saw that

I was not the most credible adviser on the subject of moral turpitude and discrepancy in ages, so I stopped speaking to Hubert altogether.

Lying in bed, I could hear the creaking directly overhead. Sometimes I would hear their voices, hers hushed and submissive, Hubert's jarringly loud. I was startled each time by the authority in his.

I'd shut my eyes, shut out their sounds, and concentrate on that second lover, the one whose touch had thrilled me so.

FOREIGN EXCHANGE
by Annie Wolff

Elaine had come through her divorce in exceptionally good shape. Everyone said so – her friends, her relatives, even her therapist. Most wives fast skidding to forty who were left for a woman fifteen years their junior would have experienced at least temporary paralysis.

There had been the initial shock, but she never went through a period of self-abasement ("*I* should feel guilty about that skunk slinking off with that skank?" she had said to her therapist, who had raised one eyebrow at this out-of-character remark. "It's all right. I'm all right," Elaine had soothed. "I just got carried away by alliteration.") She knew she had done her best and was satisfied that the responsibility, the failure, was not hers.

She even bypassed the phase of feeling wholly unattractive. Her breasts weren't firm like those of a twenty-four-year-old – like "the chippy's," as her former mother-in-law so endearingly put it. There were lines like tree rings on her buttocks, little cobwebs at the sides of her mouth and corners of her eyes, but these lines did not make her undesirable, they only underscored her value which had, she told her sister, increased with time.

She had reassurances of her continuing ability to attract men. Steadfastly single old acquaintances sought her company. Husbands of close friends offered to fill her void. Occasionally someone would begin to show serious interest in the future. She was adept at turning the conversation gently, leaving things unsaid, making it possible to continue in relationships devoid of awkward expectations.

She was quite comfortable with her social life, with life in general. Her financial settlement was enough so that in midlife she didn't have to enroll in cosmetology school or learn data entry. She continued to live in the same comfortable old house with her three children, to engage in the same volunteer activities, to attend the same cultural events. In a sense, she told the therapist, her settlement was supplemented by the meals and tickets and gifts purchased by her courtly escorts.

In many ways her life was basically unchanged. In some ways it was appreciably better. She enjoyed male attention and was receiving more of it than she had in her entire tired marriage. She enjoyed her children, now more than ever as she no longer had to act as a buffer between them and their father. She enjoyed her new flexibility – she didn't think of it as freedom or independence. She couldn't imagine giving up this life of even pleasures for the discordance of marriage, the irritation of two personalities perpetually rubbing against each other.

The only ripple she felt in her glass-smooth serenity was sexual. She did miss the comfortable regularity and predictability of her marriage bed. She had permitted herself to be drawn into two sexual relationships since her husband's departure. The first had been physically unsatisfying and she had wondered if all such encounters were doomed, if after seventeen years with the same partner she wasn't rather like an old shoe, broken in and adapted, fit only to be worn by that one lost lover.

Her second experience proved otherwise. She found not only pleasure in the union but passion as well. She was, briefly, deliriously happy, a graying teenager delighted with the delight they found in each other.

The relationship became intimate and then insistent. His qualifications were all in order: similar social background, success in his career, shared interests, affection for her children. When he volunteered to accompany her family to church on Easter morning, Elaine panicked. As though she had stepped out of a dim, curtained café and off the curb into harsh noon light, she was blindsided by the realization that her steps were taking her down a one-way petal-strewn bridal path. She ended the relationship badly, cutting him out of her life. Her children missed him and she found it impossible to explain to him or them the reasons for this elective surgery.

Elaine found that foregoing physical contact didn't result in having to forego social contact. Some men admired her for what they perceived to be quaint virtue; others in this era of sexually transmitted death respected her caution.

She never lied to herself, told herself that she wasn't missing anything, but she comforted herself that what she missed she missed by choice. And she took pains to provide other compensations, little luxuries, sensual gratifications. She lingered in shops over cheeses or bed linens or exotic coffees. She daydreamed about acquiring a servant. (Even the most careful budgeting – and Elaine didn't want the restrictions of a most careful budget – would have made the cost of live-in help burdensome.)

After some weeks' deliberation she made the half-mile journey from her front door to the university's foreign student center and offered the third floor of her house in exchange for the services of a graduate student. A child, she thought, then, a contemporary of her ex-husband's girlfriend. She filled out the colored index cards outlining the cooking, cleaning, and yard work she expected in return for room and board and went home to wait for applicants.

Two distinct images vied in her imagination. The first was of a cheerful, musical Central American girl, politically sensitive, determined to use her education and connections upon return to her native country. The other was of an Asian, a slight man-boy of indeterminate age, an Indian padding silently about, the only trace he left being the things accomplished in his wake. He would remain in the States, trading his invisible houseboy's jacket for the visible one of a radiologist or pathologist. She favored the Indian.

Eight days passed since she had made last-minute application at the housing office. The semester had begun and the students must be settled by now. She decided she was more relieved than disappointed at the failure of her Indian to materialize. He would not, after all, be a simple luxury but a complex one.

It wasn't until all hope was extinguished that she was able to respond thoughtlessly, carelessly, to the ringing of the telephone. The voice was thin and the English precise. It was the precision rather than any accent that gave it a foreign edge. He asked if the position was still open, if he might interview for it that afternoon.

Simply *meeting* him didn't obligate her.

He sat straight, formal but unstrained, not at all the woolly American type of graduate student. They discussed the terms and, when Werner found them "most acceptable," she realized a decision had been made.

There followed no real period of adjustment. In addition to some cooking and light cleaning duties – a woman came in once a week to do the floors and such – Werner discovered for himself the odd jobs which needed tending to. He planed the stubborn door of the first-floor bathroom, mended the rattling sash of the study window, raked and composted the dead sea of leaves in the front and back yards.

Each night that she stayed home or returned before he closeted himself in his room, he would tap on her bedroom door to bid her goodnight. She found the gesture charming and took those opportunities to thank him not only for his execution but also for his insight into what needed to be done.

The children liked Werner. He treated them as they wished to be treated and in return they respected his privacy.

Werner was a conscientious student as well as a conscientious house worker. Elaine worried that this left little time for a social life. She would recommend particular gallery exhibits or concerts and Werner would unfailingly thank her, but she didn't know if he ever followed any of her suggestions. Periodically she would remind him that he could entertain his friends at the house. Again Werner would thank her and the subject would be closed.

Her own friends reacted warily to the fact of Werner. The men eyed him uncomfortably while the women posed a variety of questions.

"How do you know he won't disappear some night with all your silver and your Chagall print?"

"Does he *mem sahib* you when no one's around, or is that just for company?"

"Does he do windows? Breakfast in bed? Does he do anything in bed?"

She was surprised by the questions at first. Werner's mannered reserve seemed to illuminate the chinks in her own circle's decorum.

It was her custom to plan many of her evenings out around the two nights each week that her children spent with their father. It wasn't that she disliked being alone, or that on other evenings she didn't trust them to govern themselves – her oldest boy was fifteen and a responsible babysitter – but that she enjoyed being home with them. After Werner's third month she altered her habits, not consciously at first.

One Friday evening, when Elaine's plans were unexpectedly cancelled, Werner made a fire and they read across from each other in the living room. Werner sat with open text in hand, spiral notebook and pen in lap; she was racing through a collection of Ring Lardner stories. Twice she laughed aloud and he looked up but she shook her head, helpless to convey the humor. She wondered if his meticulous English were up to the remark that Werner's jottings underscored the salient points in his reading as her laugh italicized the pointed sallies in hers. It occurred to her that she wanted to impress him.

This scene was repeated with no marked variations when her children were with her ex-husband the following Tuesday. The next week Elaine declined all invitations to go out. On the Friday after that, Werner left the house wishing her a pleasant evening, offering no explanation for his departure. Elaine spent the time wandering restlessly from one room to another, annoyed with herself and her disappointment.

She suddenly realized that she had no idea what he thought of her. It was strange thinking of him as a man, rather than as a student or an employee. He was attractive in the way his voice was attractive: his body was angular, precise; his features were clearly defined, severe even. He seemed to her complete, self-contained, without need.

When he returned that night, the light from her bedside lamp washed underneath the door into the hall. He tapped twice, softly so as not to disturb even the lightest sleep. She beckoned him in and he asked if there was anything he might do for her before he retired. She hesitated, conventions failing her, finally saying the one word "Yes." Werner stood a few moments in the doorway, not fool enough to wonder at her meaning nor boy enough to act the fool, but considering. He stepped in, closed the door behind him and made precise, though not perfunctory, love to her.

The new arrangement seemed to suit both parties. In the beginning she wondered if he had not simply found another area in which he could accommodate her. Eventually she accepted that the situation served him as well: he was a serious student who couldn't afford the time that being in love with anyone would exact.

Once their discreet pattern was well established she resumed her customary social activities. The children remained innocent of Werner's expanded duties. He slept in their mother's room only on nights they were away.

Elaine grew fond of Werner. Physically, all her restraint gradually fell away. They shared a kind of intimacy, playful, relaxed, yet somehow regulated. Regulated by schedules, yes, but also by the nature of their conversations, the subjects never touched. The past was occasionally dipped into, the well of early childhood. The present filled their talk – the behavior of the children, her steering the hospital's fundraising committee, his impressions of the university and of life in the American Midwest. The future did not exist for them.

She knew he was here for only a year's study; it had been announced on that first afternoon. As the second semester drew to a close she thought of asking him when he would be leaving, but she asked nothing. One night when the children were sleeping at their father's, Werner tapped, as he still did even against her now-open door, and entered the room where she was waiting.

"I am packed," he said.

She watched him undress, conscious of each gesture being hers to see for the last time. "Tomorrow?" she said.

"After the children come home. I should like to say goodbye."

"Why didn't you tell me before?"

His silence reproached her.

"I think they should have been prepared," she amended. "They'll miss you very much. Especially Ben."

The next day Werner took both affectionate and gravely formal farewells of the children. The younger boy fled tearfully to his room, slamming the door upon his hurt and embarrassment. With her older son and daughter she walked Werner to the taxi where he turned and gave her his hand and no forwarding address.

The house was suddenly too big. She could feel them all rattling around in it like four tiny peas in an oversized pod. And the house was too small. They tripped over each other, were caught by flying elbows and downcast looks.

The summer passed with Elaine keeping more to herself, declining most invitations, refusing to serve on boards. On the hottest day of mid-August she went to the sideboard in the dining room and poured herself the first midmorning drink of her life, then she changed into a comfortable pair of shoes and mounted the stairs.

"When the family dog is run over by a car, you should wait a while and then go out and get yourself a puppy," she whispered as she surveyed the empty third-floor rooms. At the front door, she pulled on her gardening hat to shield her from the sun.

The secretary at the foreign students' housing office hesitated over Elaine's application and Elaine cursed herself for the bouquet of whiskey on her breath. She was certain that the girl had mistaken her for the wrong sort of woman.

} PARINGS {

It was strange to return to this place of childhood, which I remembered darkly. It had seemed to me back then that everyone was always hungry, always suspicious. People wore too many clothes and still they could never get warm. Everything was heavy – the coats, the shoes, the sky, the hearts. The old country was sculpted this way, too, in the memory of my parents and my sisters: a cold, dark, empty place that could not be filled.

The only son, I had been awarded the melancholy commission of representing the family at my grandmama's funeral, while she had been charged with forestalling death until my arrival. Though she had failed by four full days, I found the town of my birth and her death not somber at all but vivid and lively.

A bright intensity could be heard in the entreaties of shopkeepers, even a keenness to the whistling of the knife sharpener as though he knew the secret of honing more than metal blades. The voices of children, rising and falling in triumph and defeat, the song of the white-kerchiefed girl who sold bunches of watercress in the street like violets – there was always something to hold one fast, something that made it hard to turn away.

They had delayed the burial until my coming, filling the coffin with pine needles and sealing it when the body of the old woman began to ripen. I had not seen my grandmama since I was nine and I felt cheated of seeing her, alive or dead, again. I knew my parents would be disappointed when they learned of this omission and perhaps even blame me for the time it takes to cross an ocean. I was lamenting such injustice to my aunt, who hushed me. Look over there, she said, at Anna. She is the spitting image of your grandmama. When you go home, you tell your parents that your eyes rested peacefully on your grandmother's face. It will be the truth, as much as there is truth in anything.

My eyes settled willingly on my cousin Anna's face. I had not realized my grandmama was so beautiful. Her eyes were as dark as pitch, her mouth a crimson wound in bronzed flesh. Heavy umber hair tumbled down her back in a swirling tumult that ended just above her pinched waist. I never wanted to look away and now my aunt had given me leave to indulge my yearning. I decided to extend my visit.

At first only my eyes were filled with Anna. Then my nose greedily drew her scent into me. Even the smell of her sweat as we labored side by side in the field was as perfume. Hungry for the sound of her voice, my ears slyly caught each exchange between Anna and the villagers. And at last in my dreams my other senses had their way. At night, when all slept, I knew the sweet, melony taste and touch of her.

In the late afternoons my cousin Anna and her brother Bruno would set out, he on a bicycle pushing a cart before it and she walking along beside him. The cart held the root vegetables that were the family's chief source of income. The whole family farmed the vegetables but only Bruno and Anna delivered them.

Others sold the same fare but could not command the same price. It was said that Bruno's fine shoulders curried favor with cooks and wives while Anna turned the heads of the innkeeper and shop owners, the men of property. But it was not just the handsome appearance of the brother and sister that made their produce appear more handsome – the pair had devised a strategy for selling the family's crops. As Bruno pedaled slowly, Anna would strut by his side, wielding a small, sharp knife with one hand upon a vegetable held firmly in the other. All who bought from them and paid their price received a vegetable sculpture created by Anna's nimble fingers.

As she walked she might fashion a trembling rabbit from a turnip or a clever squirrel out of a beet. Small children and grown men alike had been seen to clap their hands in delight at Anna's artistry. It wasn't just the novelty of her work but that her craft was so cunning. I wondered if any of her root sculptures were ever eaten as I could not conceive of the wings of her butterfly being torn apart by teeth or the head of her warbling nightingale cruelly bitten off. I imagined Anna's creatures living on unscathed until they became too shriveled to grace a table or amuse a child.

Day after day I walked some distance behind the cart and bicycle; others walked nearer, craning their necks to glimpse the newest woodland creature as it emerged. I marveled at Anna's ability to control the knife as she moved along over dirt or cobblestones. Even once when she lost her footing and slipped to the rough pavement, the mountain goat she had been carving remained unharmed. As she rose, she held up the whittled potato for all to see and applaud. So fierce was the expression, so fine the nostrils that it seemed a failing of Anna's that the tiny creature could not bleat.

I was to leave soon. A letter had come from Amerika questioning my prolonged absence and reminding me of my responsibilities. I approached Bruno and asked if by doing myself a favor I might do a favor for him as well. Bruno gestured for me to continue. I suggested that he might take the next afternoon and do whatever he pleased while I would take his cart and bicycle and accompany Anna on their customary rounds.

He said he could see the benefit to himself but what was in it for me? A ride, I told him, and that seemed to satisfy his limited curiosity.

When we set out, Anna posed no questions to me. Her curiosity was even less than Bruno's or else she understood me without asking. At any rate, my presence seemed not to distract her. Even when I spoke to her, she seldom replied. I could see she was not angry but that she only spoke when necessary, using words sparingly, as though there existed a finite number of them in her keeping. So I was all the more mindful of her sudden breaking of the silence when she asked me if it was true that I would be leaving the village soon. I acknowledged that it was my duty to depart very soon on the overland part of my journey, that if I delayed much longer my boat ticket would expire. Filling my chest with dignity, I explained I was needed to help in our small button factory where we sliced mother-of-pearl into shimmering discs to adorn ladies' dresses. Anna stood still and said is it also true your Amerika boasts highways leading away from every village while my poor country has only rivers? Proudly, I described the land of gleaming automobiles and the yawning, smooth boulevards that accommodate them. Fingering the wooden buttons on her middy, she asked if there would be room for her small person on the big boat that was to carry me away. I was amazed at the question. Could she be in earnest? What must it signify? Did it mean she loved me?

I told her I was certain a ticket could be had if there be means of purchase but, alas, I had no such means; my return ticket had been paid for, with great hardship, before I left home. How much? she stopped walking and looked directly at me. I named the sum and she looked away. I pledged I would scrape and pinch until I had saved the money for her passage, no matter if it took me the rest of my life. As long as all that, she said and sighed. She shook her head. It would only take a word from you, I pleaded. Then I must give you no word more, she returned, tossing her head and setting her chin.

She placed the mouse she had been whittling out of a large radish upon the cart. With ears alert and tail aloft, it looked so lifelike that passersby offered to purchase the mouse on the spot, but Anna turned their bids away. The plump innkeeper, whom I had watched watching Anna in the preceding weeks, proposed buying our entire cartload of vegetables if only he might have the mouse as well. I began to unload the cart but Anna signaled me to halt. She handed the mouse to the innkeeper, silently refusing to take money in exchange or to sell him any of the load of vegetables.

Looking over the produce, she selected a long-necked parsnip and from it fashioned a deep-throated lily as she walked on, letting the parings fall by the wayside. Villagers gasped at the delicacy of this new creation. Anna now chose a rutabaga with firm pale orange flesh and from it slowly carved a chain of magically interlocking flowers, a wreath that when finished was somehow three times larger in circumference than the rude vegetable from which it had come. People poured out of shops and cottages to see what could cause such excitement.

In the past Anna had made only animals. These were charming to be sure but the flower carvings were something else entirely. Before, her little creatures looked astonishingly like those made by the hand of God, but these flowers were a blasphemy, for they were, all agreed uneasily, more beautiful than the flowers in God's domain.

Soon the narrow streets swelled with villagers who followed as Anna marched on, spinning sunlit flowers out of roots that had fattened to ripeness in the cold and dark of the earth. She took a potato and turned it into a fantastic bloom, part starburst, part peony. Why had not God thought of that? She made jaunty tulip buds out of cloddish carrots and petaled roses from layered onions as the tears streamed down her cheeks.

Anna carved as she wordlessly traipsed over the cobblestone path leading to the old stone bridge that traversed the river. The crowd followed, exclaiming at each new sculpture. She remained intent, as though she walked alone, as though the cart dogged her steps riderless, like a loyal hound.

The cart was gloriously laden now with its heap of blossoms. When we reached the bridge, Anna picked up the last turnip and began its transformation into such perfectly waxen white petals that some of the onlookers claimed they could smell the heady scent of the gardenia. After finishing this final flower, Anna placed it carefully on top of the others and then climbed onto the arch of the bridge. The crowd jostled and hushed each other, expecting Anna to address them. I, too, became still.

Without a backward glance, still silent, Anna jumped from the bridge at its highest point, into the swirling waters below. Many of the witnesses surged onto the bridge, shouting her name, as if to call her back. The water took her down and held her fast against the pilings until she had renounced her struggle. Then, like a cork that has been forced down into a bottle, her body popped up to the water's surface.

She belonged to the river now. I was embarrassed that I had thought she might belong to me. For all my watching and dreaming, I never knew the first thing about her. I pushed the cart up onto the decaying bridge and dropped the gardenia over the side. The river carried the bloom to her.

One by one, the mourners filed past the cart, each sending a flower down to her mutable grave. No dark earth would ever hold her. When the interlaced pale rutabaga flowers were captured by the current, the wreath became perfectly entangled in her long, streaming hair. As we watched, the fast, jealous river carried her on her bier of blossoms far away, at last, from the village.

I sailed the next week, over the dread water, to the family I had left behind. They said I was changed. I could not contradict them. I brought them the story of missing the passing of my grandmama but being present for that of my cousin whose face was said to be the same. But how can I tell them I found my cousin Anna's funeral more vital an occasion than any celebration of life that has come after?

I have never felt as deeply for another woman. Perhaps that was the fate Anna chose for me because, even so, callow and dull as I was, I could not feel deeply enough. I care for my wife and my sons and my daughter, who has the dark, drowning eyes of her great-grandmother and her distant cousin, but it is an easy sort of sentiment, as life is easy in this new country of broad, smooth streets and tamed waterways.

} DANCE OF THE HOURS {

"Divorce her," Nicole pleaded to her husband. "You've divorced the two mothers of your children. Breaking away from Sally should be easy by comparison. You deserve a little peace."

"She's old." Adam fiddled with his wedding ring, removing and replacing the incised gold band. "She doesn't have anybody else."

"Age doesn't have anything to do with it and you know it – she's always been this way. And of course she doesn't have anybody else. Not because you're an only child, but because she's...impossible." When Nicole was trying to explain this mother-son relationship to her therapist, she said, "Sally comes into the room and I can read the Cartesian variation playing in Adam's head: 'I cringe, therefore I am.'"

} {

"Give it a rest, please, Nicole."

She knew he meant *Give me* a rest. Her voice softened, "Divorce her, Adam, so I won't have to divorce you." Adam understood her words not as a threat but a genuine expression of fear. True, Sally had aimed poisonous barbs at all her daughters-in-law, but it was the undercutting of her son that had proved fatal to his marriages.

He stopped by his mother's house each Sunday morning to help with her bills, balance her checkbook, replace light bulbs, and eat a slab of the Entenmann's coffee cake she forced on him. Under the guise of reminiscing, Sally seized these opportunities to rake up his past, reminding him of the performance award he had won at Julliard or the patent lawyer his first wife had left him for.

After one of these visits with his mother, Adam might plunge into a dry spell of anywhere from a single day to several months where he didn't try to create music, periods when he didn't trust himself to have anything left worth offering. Nicole would point to his successes but, when he was in these spells, such praise only confirmed that his achievements were relegated to the past. Eventually he would return to the piano, but these episodes of doubt weakened him. Nicole feared the effects to be cumulative. That's why she felt unrepentantly relieved when Adam finally agreed his mother had to be sent to a nursing home.

Neither illness nor senility had captured Sally but infirmity had taken hold. She had trouble with stairs, with lifting pans and turning off faucets, with putting on her shoes. And the house reflected her limitations.

Sally kept multiple cigarettes going simultaneously. Adam had given up trying to get her to quit. She boasted her lungs would probably collapse if they received a higher ratio of oxygen than customary. Her idea of doing something healthful in the way of smoking was to switch to mentholated brands when she had a cough or sore throat.

Sally didn't abandon her smokes promiscuously; it just took her too long to navigate from the table to the stove to go without a drag, and she couldn't manage carrying a cigarette and the coffee pot at the same time. The day had to come when she left a lit cigarette in the living room while she enjoyed another in the bathroom. Just as she'd finished her business in there, the phone rang – someone trying to sell her burial insurance – and she never made it back to the living room. Six hours later, after the firefighters had left and the neighbors had tracked Adam down at a recording session, he arrived to chauffeur Sally and a few necessities back to their house until "a suitable arrangement" could be made. This didn't require nearly as much time as Sally anticipated because Nicole had been scouting nursing homes for over a year.

Sally tried refusing to go.

Nicole didn't want to inflict needless pain, but she wasn't going to avoid the necessary. "You can't stay alone," she said crisply.

But Sally had already stopped insisting she be allowed to return home. She could see even Adam was unmovable on that score. "I could stay here." There was nothing of the supplicant about her as she said this. If anything, a steely glint shone in her eyes.

"I'm sorry," Nicole said, equally flinthearted, "you know that's not possible."

A room became available at one of the better "assisted living" residences a few days before Mother's Day. Adam and Nicole decided to take Sally for a Mother's Day brunch to the café at the art museum and then on to the nursing home from there. The director said the staff preferred morning admissions but he made an exception in their case.

Sally dressed for the occasion. She wore a bright pink shift with Eiffel Towers careening across the fabric at all angles. Nicole imagined she looked like the kind of hallucination produced by a mind in the throes of delirium tremens: an Erector Set-encrusted, Pepto Bismol-coated elephant. As often happened, Nicole had to restrain herself from asking her mother-in-law where (in God's name) she had purchased her outfit.

At the end of the meal, after Sally read her card and unwrapped the box holding the handpainted silk shawl, she asked, eyes blinking either in incredulity or from the smoke of her cigarette (which both the waiter and café hostess had asked her to extinguish), "This the latest thing in geriatric wear – no snaps, no buttons, no shape?"

"Do you like it?" Adam asked rhetorically, his left eye twitching rapidly.

"We bought it from the artist," Nicole interceded.

"Is that so? I guess that makes this what they call 'wearable art'? In my day wearable art was a sandwich board. I predict the next new craze will be 'flushable art.' You heard it here." She waved her cigarette grandly in the air above her head, like a Fourth of July sparkler.

"I'm sorry you don't like it," Nicole shouldered the liability.

"I didn't say that. Did I say that?" she turned to her son, seeking acknowledgment that his wife was trying to put words in her mouth. "I was just hoping for something a little more personal from my only son for Mother's Day."

Like a garter belt? Nicole bit the inside of her cheek to keep from snapping. Sally had the knack of getting her to conceive thoughts that were totally out of character.

"Like a song from my famous composer son," Sally corrected as if Nicole had spoken aloud. "One little sheet of sheet music."

Adam winced. "Hardly famous." He wasn't aware that he was chewing on his tongue.

"False modesty is so unbecoming," his mother smiled flirtatiously. "The women in my bridge group were always telling me about concerts they go to where they hear your music. They're always congratulating me."

"How tedious for you," Nicole said tonelessly and turned away to avoid the look Adam sent in her direction.

"How about a ditty for your mother? Hum a few bars of your latest."

Adam, who belonged to the New Music Circle and composed primarily avant-garde chamber music, sat paralyzed by the word "ditty."

"How about the check?" Nicole said loud enough for the hovering waiter to overhear. With one hand he presented their bill, already totaled, while with the other he whisked Sally's bread plate away, with its hash of crumbs and butter and ash and still-smoldering butt.

} {

Nicole had reserved space for her mother-in-law at Briarcliff, a facility with the jaunty air and overstuffed chairs of a country club. Sally moved into a private room in the "ambulatory" division. Residents were encouraged to participate in classes and activities. "Every Tuesday evening there's a live concert in the lounge," Nicole told Adam. "Mostly guest performers, but sometimes one of the residents. There's a woman who used to teach violin at the conservatory and she plays occasionally. You should get on the schedule. Your mother can show you off to her new neighbors."

Nicole was happier than she could recall, but she refrained from saying so. The same was true for Adam, though he, too, kept any unseemly jubilation to himself. The only one clearly unsatisfied with the new arrangement was Sally and she wasted no time in letting everyone know exactly how she felt.

"I'm afraid your mother isn't very pleased to be staying with us," the young social director apologized to Nicole a month into Sally's stay. "I thought she'd settle in by now."

"My husband's mother," Nicole corrected. She touched the social director's arm confidingly, "My mother-in-law has never been the cheerful sort, but I'm afraid my husband still takes responsibility for her moods."

"I understand," the young woman said, agreeing to the conspiracy. "I've learned from this job that some people make the best of a situation and others take the same situation and make the worst of it. We mustn't let your husband blame himself for that."

As long as Sally was complaining, Nicole was serene. Complaints from Sally were to be expected. At last their lives were reasonably predictable.

Because there were no long lists of real and invented household chores to attend to, Adam now made all his visits to his mother on the fly. On the way to the dentist. Before a meeting. Between rehearsals. There was never enough time for Sally to rummage in his past, stick her probing hands into his memories. When Sally would raise her voice like a hatchet above his head, cursing the place – the food, the employees, the "inmates" – Adam would cock his head sympathetically and urge his mother to "Give it time," as he eased himself out of her presence, backing away as though she were royalty or a carrier of some dread disease.

But Nicole grew wary when, several months into her sojourn at Briarcliff, Sally became unusually quiet. "Maybe she's starting to feel at home," Adam said with uncharacteristic optimism. Nicole decided not to probe. Let sleeping bitches lie, she told herself, amazed at the intemperate thoughts Sally could provoke in her otherwise temperate brain. Then came the visit from Mrs. Archibald Spencer Hunt.

Mrs. Hunt would have made an ideal mother-in-law. Nicole knew her as the secretary of the Historical Society board. Soft-spoken, rail thin, and not at all inquisitive, she was thorough in her recording of minutes and genial when they had worked together on the capital campaign committee. And she had never, within Nicole's sight, committed a fashion offense, except the occasional mixing of plaids the American aristocracy was strangely prone to.

Nicole was distressed by Mrs. Hunt's distress. "Are you sure?" she asked delicately.

"I saw them," Mrs. Hunt said, her voice tremulous.

Nicole drove to Briarcliff that afternoon. She found Sally in her room watching *Wheel of Fortune*, a fiercely chewed plastic pen dangling from the corner of her mouth. After a long silence Nicole blurted, "Mrs. Archibald Hunt came over this morning."

"Oh? I expect she's lonely." Sally's eyes remained fixed on Vanna White.

Nicole jabbed the power button on the television set. "She was very upset." She steeled herself to continue. "She says you're having an affair with her husband."

"Archie? Well, I suppose I am."

"My God." She had, of course, believed Mrs. Hunt, but she had expected Sally to deny it. "How could you, Sally?"

"You insert tab A into slot B. Haven't you and Adam figured it out yet?"

"The man has Alzheimer's."

"Nobody's perfect."

"He's not competent."

"You won't hear any complaints from me."

"It's disgusting."

"Then don't you think about it." She slapped her palm on the arm of her La-Z-Boy emphatically, in support of closing the subject.

"You realize this is like rape. He's not responsible. I'm sure it's against the law."

"So, sue me."

Nicole grappled with herself. "Try for a moment to imagine how Mrs. Hunt feels."

"You try imagining how Archie felt when she dumped him here."

"This is a perfectly lovely place. He's very lucky they'll accept people like that."

"I'll tell him you said so."

"I'll have to tell Adam."

"Is that what you do with Adam? Talk dirty to him?"

} {

Sally had tricked her husband into marrying her. Not by the common ruse of pretending to be pregnant with his child, but by pretending to be impregnated by his music.

A secretary in the chemistry department, she had been taken to a campus concert by one of the graduate students. They sat in the seventh row, where Sally had been mesmerized by the young pianist's balletic hands, their authoritativeness and grace. She was particularly taken with his hand-over-hand flourishes, their suggestion of eternal motion.

She had no idea what piece he had played or if he had played well. She hadn't looked at the program except to scan the soloists' biographical notes in search of his name. Van Dillen. Van, she imagined herself breathing as those fingers played on the buttons of her dress. "Van," she sighed under cover of applause. It was the name of a leading man: Van Heflin. Van Johnson. And even a leading pianist, she reminded herself: Van Cliburn. It wasn't until they were applying for the marriage license that she learned he'd been born George van Dillen. George was the name of her uncle who was a vendor at the baseball stadium. She went into City Hall with a Van and emerged with a George so, in a way, he had tricked her into marrying him too.

At the party following the concert, Sally had introduced herself with a gushing "You are magnificent." Van was seduced by her use of the present tense. She seemed able to detect an artistry that persisted beyond his performance. That evening Sally was wearing a jade chiffon sheath strained enticingly across her hourglass shape, setting off her hazel eyes and chestnut hair, but it was her praise Van succumbed to.

It wasn't long before they realized the marriage had been a mistake, a union of oil and water, of fire and ice, but by that time Sally had become pregnant with Adam.

"Some people live in harmony," Van said, trying for perspective, "some in discord. Our performance is in counterpoint." He wanted her to relax with him into resignation.

"Spare me, maestro," she had said, the rage beginning to accumulate. "This isn't a prelude, this is my life."

} {

There had been no trickery with Archie Hunt, just an honest exchange of bodily fluids, such as they had remaining to them. He had wandered into her room, despite her closed door, and unzipped his pants, releasing his penis, which was startlingly rosy and firm in contrast to the body it was attached to.

"God!" Sally had exclaimed involuntarily.

"Where?" Archie asked anxiously, turning to examine the four corners of the room.

Sally crossed in front of him to close the door and he smiled and said, "Geneva," as he patted her behind with his free hand. She didn't know if he was recalling a place or a person.

"Well, buster," she sighed, "what are we going to do with you?" when the answer struck her as self-evident. He continued to smile as she took him by the hand and led him to the bed.

Afterward, she congratulated herself on her decades of continued masturbation, keeping her hand in the game, so to speak.

} {

On their first anniversary, Sally, already pregnant but not yet showing, tried to shove her marriage off its unswerving trajectory. While Van was practicing at the piano, Sally was equally busy in the bedroom, drawing part of a keyboard along her left flank with an eyeliner pencil. She outlined the ivory keys and filled in the black and then waited for a lull in the next room before summoning her husband.

"Happy anniversary," she purred like a starlet when he appeared at the door. She threw off the sheet covering her opulent body. "Play me." She hadn't known what to expect. That had been her chief incentive.

He seemed frozen at first, but then edged toward her. Sitting cross-legged on the bed, he lowered his left hand to execute a chord.

"Go on," she encouraged.

"There aren't enough keys," he apologized.

"Play *me*," she urged softly.

"Silly," he said and bent to kiss her on the nose before extricating himself.

} {

At the age of forty-seven Van suffered a cerebral aneurism that left him paralyzed on one side. As much as she had come to hate her rival, that much she had to pity her husband who could no longer retreat into his playing. He was as bereft as she had been throughout their marriage. In contrast to the tight control he had always displayed as a performer and as a husband, he was subject to crying fits. She told the doctors, without malice, that if they found a way to let him go it would be a mercy. She would never know if it was this suggestion or the pneumonia that had finally done him in.

Van had died early but not soon enough. The club the Dillen men had formed would never admit Sally. It wasn't just music they shared but a sensibility. As they cultivated refinement, Sally grew more coarse, flesh thickening, voice roughened by years of tobacco use, discourse bordering on the crude.

She supposed there had been an ample number of ideal mates out there for her husband had he been free. Long before her arrival at the nursing home, she fixed on the notion that any one of Adam's proper, prissy wives would have served Van perfectly.

There might have been some joy for her in the grandchildren, but those haughty bitches had clutched their offspring to them, circling the wagons against her, the ignoble savage. And Adam had tacitly approved.

She would never forgive him. She'd made him pay, week after week, for that ultimate disloyalty. She had carried him in her body. She had even stopped smoking for the duration of the pregnancy, decades before it became a moral imperative. She had changed his diapers, washed his clothes, clipped his nails, wiped his nose, prepared his meals, gone on school field trips. Motherhood had been a thankless job.

} {

The first time Sally had taken notice of Archie was at the most memorable of the Tuesday evening musicales. She had started attending these because she was restless after dinner, and she would shuffle out midway through for the same reason.

This night she picked up a copy of the program, a folded sheet of paper printed with the names of the performers from the Marymount School and the two pieces they would play. She studied the first title, "Dance of the Hours" from Ponchielli's *La Gioconda*. It had been a continuing source of surprise and perverse gratification that, despite years of exposure, no printed name of a classical work evoked notes in her head. She couldn't conjure up the opening bars of Beethoven's *Ninth*, not by looking at the words on paper, though popular song titles brought entire melodies rushing in.

The first notes of the piece sounded and Archie's clear, strong tenor along with them: "Hello Muddah, hello Faddah. Here. I. Am. At. Camp Grenada. Camp is ver-y en-ter-taining. And-they-say-we'll-have-some-fun-if-it-stops-raining." The doorman materialized at Archie's elbow, half-lifting him out of his chair, propelling him from the lounge even as he sang.

Sally wondered if his performance wasn't the precise antidote to all the Dillen concerts she'd sat through.

The flustered girls laboring on their instruments were too young to be familiar with the Allan Sherman burlesque, but the residents were captive to the absent Archie now, hearing the notes as lumbering and oafishly comic. Those who still had their wits about them flushed guiltily.

} {

When Adam and Nicole popped in together, Sally could tell at once that Nicole hadn't said anything about Archie. Her daughter-in-law's fear of rocking the boat suited Sally just fine.

She asked Adam to buy her one of those boxy little sound systems with a radio and tape and CD players. She mentioned that her friend Archie really perked up when he was listening to music. Nicole squirmed but Adam was visibly pleased by this sign of adjustment to life at Briarcliff. He promised to make the purchase later that same day.

When he stepped out of the room to consult one of the nursing staff about Nicole's suspicion that his mother was developing Parkinson's, Sally took the opportunity to stoke her daughter-in-law's inbred uneasiness. "You know," she said sweetly, "you'd better watch out for that cross-eyed little social director. I think she's got a notion to throw her hat in the running for Mrs. Adam Dillen number four."

} {

The sound system provided welcome assistance in curbing Archie's roaming. Keeping an eye on him turned out to be a full-time occupation. Sally didn't want Archie trying to diddle someone else, and possessiveness amounted to only a fraction of the reason. Mostly she was afraid he'd be locked up or restrained or sedated if he ambled into the wrong room. Not that every female was a sexual target. Even with Sally he had to be reminded of the function of a stiffened penis.

Archie was just as likely to wander into one of the men's bedrooms. When word went round that Mr. Avouris's teeth had disappeared from the glass next to his bed, Sally checked the pocket of Archie's robe and found the dentures, along with a stray pair of harlequin reading glasses. She deposited the teeth in the basin of the drinking water fountain in the hallway off the lounge and tucked the glasses behind one of the pillows on an overladen loveseat. As she'd surmised, the quest to determine the identity of a culprit was dropped with the discovery of the "misplaced" objects.

At first she resented the visits of the superior Mrs. A. Spencer Hunt. On those occasions, Sally would roost in the far corner of the lounge, flipping newspaper or magazine pages while craning to keep her eyes on the door to Archie's room. Jealous of the time husband and wife spent on the other side of that closed door, she eventually reconciled herself to those visits as they usually had a calming effect on Archie. And apparently, Mrs. Hunt, like Nicole, had elected to keep Archie and Sally's trysts to herself, though this decision must have been extremely trying for her in the face of the staff's exuberant praise of Sally's solicitude toward her husband.

"How Van would have admired her," Sally mused aloud to Archie who blinked vacantly back. "Such genteel stoicism."

Mrs. A.S.H. and Sally's daughters-in-law had so much in common. After all, it had been Archie's wife and Adam's latest who'd deposited them in this sterile, smoke-free environment.

Sally had been required to quit cold turkey. That was hard, and no one gave her credit for it. You could say that Archie was her substitute for cigarettes. But there was more to it than profound physical craving. She comforted him and protected him and, while he didn't say much of anything, he never said anything to hurt her.

When asked by admirers of her husband what instrument she played, Sally had invariably drawled, "Second fiddle." Years later, responding to the same hollow question posed by the devotees of her son, she'd bark, "Instrument? Me? I'm the harpy." Wouldn't it surprise all the worshippers of those two divinities who, with their elongated fingers, could stroke passion from a cold keyboard that it was with Archie, whose mind had absconded with his memory and his manners, that she had stumbled upon something like love?

She hummed the opening bars to an old Gershwin standard – "How Long Has This Been Going On?" – and was rewarded by Archie's plaintive, "I could cry/ salty tears/ Where have I been/ all these years?" She took one closed fist in both her hands and, unfurling it, pressed his palm to her cheek. "It doesn't matter where we've been, sweetie," she said. "We're here now."

} FOR THE HOME TEAM {

The country drowsed through the languid summer of 1951. Spring had brought harsh squalls, the detonation of a hydrogen bomb at Eniwetok atoll, and the Rosenberg trial. Summer was ushered in by a gentle wind of prosperity. The coastal storms, the fallout, and the political tempest had dissipated somewhere over the vast central plains; only in Brooklyn did the climate remain disturbed. It was the summer when Billy Sarasohn and I stopped being best friends. It was the summer I was sent to Uncle Leonard's farm. It was the summer my father left and Ralph Branca pitched to Bobby Thomson.

Billy Sarasohn and I had been inseparable since the first day of first grade when, standing in the boys' line waiting for the entrance bell, we came to blows over somebody's shoes – his or mine, I can't remember. For six years we walked to school together. Billy came by the apartment and stayed for breakfast every weekday morning. My father sat with the *Daily Mirror* spread over half the undersized table while my mother, Billy, and I huddled around the other half.

My father would hurl questions at Billy that he had asked of me the night before: "Who discovered the North Pole? What's the square root of 121? What was the final score between the Dodgers and the Braves in their 1920 26-inning game?" For each incorrect or tardy response he penalized us by taking something off our plates. Sometimes, if my mother fixed something special, a strudel say, he made the questions impossible.

I don't think we were ever quite sure what we thought of the game but we knew we weren't competing just for food. I would stop chewing and wait to hear if Billy could come up with an answer that I couldn't the night before. As soon as we got out the door we would compare scores. We kept a running total and stayed fairly even. Billy outdid me in geography and history, but I led in math, current events, and baseball.

That summer Billy told me he had seen his father and my mother kissing and touching in the back room of the store where his father worked as a butcher. I said I didn't believe it – his father was probably just helping my mother with her coat or something.

A few days later Billy came by for breakfast. School was out by then, but that didn't matter to my father: "Who pitched the last game of the 1947 Series? What's the capital of Arizona? What were the Wright brothers' first names?" Billy missed two out of three and had both pieces of toast snatched from his plate.

"I know more than you think," Billy said, looking at my mother, then his eyes fell to his empty plate. "I know more than you do," he burst into tears. I was amazed to see Billy cry. We were twelve years old and didn't do that any more. No one else seemed startled. My father kept nodding at him, my mother just went white. Billy left, wiping his eyes on the shoulder of his striped cotton T-shirt, while we sat on silently in the kitchen. It seemed that Billy's words, which could have meant nothing to my parents, meant everything to them.

Less than a week later I was packed off to New Jersey to spend the summer on Uncle Leonard and Aunt Judith's farm. Leonard was my mother's older brother whose marriage had never produced children. My father told Leonard he should stop trying to grow things, animal or vegetable, and stick to mineral. He said Leonard was a natural salesman who could coax silver out of a poor man's pocket quicker than he could a weed out of the richest soil. Every year Uncle Leonard and Aunt Judith invited me to the barren farm for school vacation. Every year I prayed my parents would not make me go and every year my prayers were heard, until the summer of 1951. God went stone deaf and I was exiled from Brooklyn.

I packed and repacked my suitcase: shirts, pants, books, autographed fielder's mitt – none of them suited to life on the farm. I stopped at Billy's to say goodbye but his mother said he wasn't around so I walked down to the candy store. Billy might be there but anyway I needed to lay in a supply for the duration. Who could trust New Jersey to stock Black Jack gum?

John sat behind the counter, belly resting on the edge, in what looked like the same white, short-sleeved shirt with yellow stains under the arms that he wore every day, winter and summer. He knew exactly where everything in the store was without ever turning his head. John never had to get up to find anything for a customer.

I was covering the countertop with all that I could get for the last of my birthday money. I figured there'd be no place to spend it around the farm anyway.

"Hey, big spender."

"Hey, yourself."

"Who you tryin' to impress?"

"My dentist."

"Got a sweetheart with a sweet tooth, I bet. No girl's worth your whole wad, Daniel. I didn't figure you for such a pushover."

"It's all for me."

"What – you plan on not coming back 'til you're old enough to vote? I'd sure miss your unsmiling face."

"I'm going to my uncle's farm for the summer."

"Can't take it, huh?" Still motionless, John called out to a kid two aisles away, "An' you better not take what you got in your hand, Joey. I got eyes you ain't even seen yet."

"Take what, John?"

"Hanging around while the Giants cream the Dodgers. I get it. You'll be back when the season's over and you figure you won't have to apologize for those shuffling bums. That's a Dodger fan for you."

I pictured the weight of John's stomach finally breaking through the glass countertop, sending jagged missiles and colorful explosions of Jujubes and Snaps and Red Hots everywhere.

"Hey, Mrs. Sandler," he called over my shoulder, "remember the last game of the season? Dodgers played the Whiz Kids to break the tie going into the playoffs and the Phillies made cream cheese out of them. Point is, when it comes down to the wire, the Dodgers can't cut it. Right, Daniel?"

"That how much I owe you?"

"Hey, Daniel. Make me a bet. Today's game: I say Dodgers lose to St. Louis. Dodgers win and you don't hafta pay me nothin' for the candy. If St. Louis wins then you pay and run a coupla errands for me. Whaddya say?"

"I'm not allowed to bet."

John sighed expansively in the direction of Mrs. Sandler. "That's a Dodger fan for you."

} {

Aunt Judith met our train. She sat with us in the station until it was time for my mother to catch the next train back to the city. They spoke quietly, as though their hushed tones would divest their words of meaning for me.

"What's going to happen now?" Aunt Judith's eyes always looked luminous and sad. Her watery gaze rested on my mother's hand repeatedly pressing a fold of pleated skirt.

"I don't know."

"Talk to him, Ruthie."

"I've tried. He won't speak to me."

"God willing, he will soften. Give him time."

"I've given him fourteen years already. He never did speak to me, you know. Now at least he's got a reason."

When I saw my mother shudder I recognized the tremor for what it was: an earthquake unsettling my world. I suddenly knew that my stay on the farm would not be an interruption of the sameness of my days, but those days would be – were already – forever altered. I didn't realize I would be walking by myself to school in the fall or that my mother would never again hover over me in her anxious, distant way – I only sensed she would have other worries to absorb her now.

They worked me hard at the farm, though no harder than Uncle Leonard would have worked the son he was cheated out of. When he told me that the pitchfork got its name because it developed the arm for curve balls, I almost believed him. Then I would remember he didn't even know who Pee Wee Reese was: "With the Barnum-Bailey circus? I got it – a clown."

Convinced I was being made to squander the best part of my youth, I practiced cursing as I shoveled drifts of chickenshit.

Chicken was the essential fact of the farm. Their smell, sight, sound, and taste gave shape to the days. Breakfast began with good brown eggs; supper was followed by creamy egg custard. Sometimes there was roasted chicken in between. Slow, sad Aunt Judith would bend to a strutting hen like a bear capturing trout from a running stream. With two deft motions so unlike her, she would wring the neck. I'd singe the feathers, holding the bird over burning newspaper. My aunt cut off the head and extracted the pinfeathers while sitting on the steps of the back porch. She removed the organs at the kitchen sink. "You have to watch out for the gall bladder," she said ritually, like a sorcerer to a dim apprentice. She scalded the feet and pulled off their skin and, with the gizzard and the heart, dropped them into the soup kettle that was always simmering at the back of the stove.

My mother came to visit once that summer. She came on the morning train and left after dinner. She was very quiet, shelling peas and chopping vegetables to be put up for relish.

"Did Billy come over?" I asked. "I wrote him a letter, but he didn't write back."

"Why would he come over when you're not there?" my mother said vacantly.

"Before," I said. "Before he knew I was gone. Before I wrote to him or somebody told him."

"Maybe somebody told him right away," she said. She dropped another onion into the meat grinder that was screwed tight to the kitchen table with its vise. As she turned the crank, onion bits streamed from the grinder and onion tears streamed from her eyes.

"Is Dad going to come? To the farm, I mean. On a visit?" I thought maybe they were taking turns. I thought maybe they each had something to tell me.

"I don't know," she said and stuffed the mouth of the grinder with more onion for Aunt Judith's piccalilli.

After she'd gone, I went into the spare bedroom which had become mine, felt banners tacked to the wall, drawings of airplanes taped above my bed, and my favorite baseball cards jammed into the wooden frame of the mirror hanging over the dresser. In the first drawer were my treasures – my mitt, an abandoned towhee nest, the rest of my baseball card collection. The middle drawer held my clothes, the third an extra blanket. I took from the top drawer the model of the *U.S.S. Saratoga* I had made from a kit my parents had given me for my birthday. I held the plastic aircraft carrier against the dresser and slammed the open drawer on it. It broke only along a glued seam.

I didn't hear from my father, or about my father, at all.

One evening Uncle Leonard asked me to build a framed screen for the entrance to the chicken house. As I placed the narrow board against the wooden miter box under his watchful eye, I thought for the first time that there must be tools for doing everything simply, correctly.

"Maybe you'll need some more help around here," I said into the dusk.

"No," my uncle complimented. "You do plenty. Isn't that so, Judith?"

"Yes, Leonard." She sat behind us on the porch swing peeling apples into a white enameled washbasin.

"I mean," I said very casually, "after school starts. Maybe I could stay. Help out."

Uncle Leonard patted the sawdust from the thighs of his pants and then looked up. "Your parents will expect you back to the City."

"They won't care. It'll probably be a relief. My father hasn't even sent me a postcard or anything."

"Sure, sure. He is stupid. I mean no disrespect. Men are stupid is all. They don't know how to act."

I was glad to find that we two were somehow excluded from this society of morons.

} {

I was seldom as lonely on the farm as I had expected. What I lacked in company my own age I made up for in quick-moving fellow boarders: lightning bugs, field mice, a pair of untemperamental goats, and the chickens full of their city chatter and schoolyard games. Besides, Aunt Judith had a radio.

It sat on the kitchen table, occupying the fourth place, an honored guest. Aunt Judith never switched the radio on when she was cooking or scouring. The camel-humped box was a dinner companion, a friend to while away the evening with.

That summer I kept up with the *Lucky Strike Hit Parade*, with *Inner Sanctum*, with the winning streak of the Dodgers, and with the errors, strikeouts, and foul balls of the Giants. I bristled at the gravelly voice of the Giants' announcer Russ Hodges and I thrilled to the words of Chuck Dressen, Brooklyn's manager, as they cackled with static: "The Giants is dead."

My aunt and uncle had never followed baseball and so they

supposed I sought consolation when I announced on August second that the Giants were 13½ games out of first place. "There's no chance they'll take the Pennant." My voice was without emotion as I contemplated all the faces of John's misery while appearing to be studying the bleached linoleum.

"There's always a chance," my uncle said. "Look at that sunset. A miracle. Hold this egg in your palm. A miracle. If God can do that, what's a little thing like a Pennant?"

The Giants' comeback that summer was nothing short of miraculous.

} {

I was back in Brooklyn in time for the National League Pennant race, but not in time to see my father move out. My aunt and uncle sent me home with jars of pickled everything and an invitation to return next summer. My mother met me with a box of Cracker Jacks and a collapsed smile. No one said anything about my father not being there.

The next day the telephone rang and my mother stood by my bedroom door. "Your father wants to talk to you."

"How was the farm?" he said.

"Fine."

"You start school soon?"

"Day after tomorrow."

"I've got two tickets for the third game of the playoffs."

"Jeepers creepers!"

"You want to go?"

"Sure!"

Easy questions. And all the right answers. I went to Billy's apartment with my summer harvest, the bow my uncle had made for me from hickory wood and the arrows I had made for myself, plumed with chicken feathers.

An old man with a wet cloth draped over his head opened the door.

"What do you want?" he said.

"I was looking for Billy. Billy Sarasohn," I added with a sure, sinking feeling.

"They moved."

"When?"

"In August. The third. They were supposed to be out by the end of July. It was not easy staying with my niece's family."

"Where did they go?"

"Do I look like an encyclopedia?"

} {

I saw my father only once before the game. He was waiting for me outside of school. From the other side of the chain link fence he said, "Everything okay?"

"Billy's gone." I had started to say "gone too" but I thought the too might be taken as criticism. "His whole family." I watched my father closely. I wasn't sure that it hadn't been his doing. "Do you know where they went?" I said.

"Do I look like an encyclopedia?"

For a second I thought maybe he and the old man were in cahoots, but no, I knew my father could never be on intimate enough terms to conspire with anybody. Later I realized I had missed my opportunity, my chance to say, "Who's supposed to be the encyclopedia around here anyway? Who's supposed to have all the answers about blown-away hurricanes and dead ballplayers?"

I missed him. Predictably, I missed him most at mealtimes. Dinner didn't taste the same now that I didn't need to defend it. Breakfast was a slow, near silent affair, without even the rustle of a newspaper.

My mother spent most of her time alone.

While I didn't blame her for my father's leaving – I had always known they didn't fit together – I was still angry with her. All those years she had failed to protect me I'd assumed she was afraid of my father. Now I saw that sticking up for me had never occurred to her.

Fortunately for us both, I was consumed with the starting lineups for the third game of the playoffs. Since the playoffs began so quickly after the regular season, the Dodgers would be hurting for pitchers. Still, Brooklyn would beat the Giants and then take the World Series. It would be on the radio, all over the papers: John would be too humiliated to show his face at the candy store. Either he would quit his job or at the very least sit satisfyingly hangdog, eyes lowered to his pitcher's mound of a belly, every time a Dodger fan came in.

The teams had to split the first two games for there to be a third. I made secret vows and wore my underwear inside out. The Giants won the first game; the Dodgers the second. Whoever took the third would take the Pennant. It was the game of the year, the game of a lifetime, and my father had seats on the third base line.

He picked me up outside the apartment in his new car, a two-tone Ford, black with yellow roof: "Just listen to this bumble bee hum." No one in the neighborhood owned a car. I felt I wasn't riding so much as being propelled into a faster, chrome-trimmed future.

The game is history. Mine. Brooklyn's. For those a few years older the question would always be "Where were you when you learned about Pearl Harbor?" For those a few years younger it would be "Where were you when you heard that Kennedy had been shot?" For us, just coming into our own in New York, the electrifying, unifying moment came in the ninth inning of the third and final game of the 1951 Dodgers-Giants playoffs. I was on my fourth hot dog at the seventh inning stretch.

"Who pitched two games apiece for Brooklyn in the 1947 Series?"

"I dunno," I said, slow with sun and food.

"Casey and Branca," my father flashed and grabbed the half hot dog from my hand. He pushed it into his mouth in one large bite, an exclamation point.

I had been wondering how I would finish that fourth dog. Suddenly I wished he would choke on it.

I thought about that, about him dying there in the stands. My mother would be a respectable widow instead of somebody whose husband moved out. And maybe Billy would come back then.

"Hey, sport," my father said, his mouth full, "you look like somebody who just lost his best friend." He jabbed my arm.

I turned away and made myself think about the game, how baseball was about waiting: the players waiting in the dugout for a turn at bat or waiting in the field for a ball that might never be hit to them. Time after time, a hundred times in a game, ten thousand times in a season, a man standing in left field readies himself to run or leap or dive and the umpire calls "Stee-rike!" And each time the left fielder stands poised, tensed, ready again. My mother would say, "How can you sit there all afternoon with nothing happening?" She would never understand that the point of the seventh inning stretch wasn't to exercise away a lethargy that had set in but to relieve the almost incessant tension of the game.

The Dodgers were leading 4-2 in the last half of the ninth when they brought in Ralph Branca to pitch to Bobby Thomson. Clem Labine was the favored relief pitcher but he had been used up in the glorious second game when the Dodgers destroyed the Giants 10-0.

The Giants needed an improbable three runs to win the game. There were two men on base, second and third. If Branca walked Thomson he would have broken the cardinal rule of never putting the winning run on base. The first pitch was a strike; the second ended my season.

Branca is remembered only for that pitch which Thomson hit into the left field stands, "the home run heard round the world." No one had foreseen it, but in a shattering instant everyone grasped what it meant. I can still hear the crack of wood. I didn't hear the roar that followed. It was over. The Giants had won, 5 to 4. I watched Thomson as he rounded third base, floating home.

Wars and plagues take years to wreak their destruction. I wasn't so lucky. In no time at all, my mother had gone from being unhappy to being miserable. My father was living alone in a mysterious rented room somewhere. My best friend had disappeared from the face of the earth, the face of Brooklyn. And now the Dodgers had lost the Pennant. And they'd lost it to the Giants.

During the ride home from the Polo Grounds I fought my tears and wondered how Billy was taking it. Not yet having learned how to separate, my father and I went for a walk around the neighborhood.

"They should have pulled Labine yesterday," I said, kicking at the sidewalk.

"Why?"

"To save his arm for today. They didn't need him in there."

"How do you think Labine would have liked it if they pulled him out of his shut-out? Besides, they had Branca. C'mon, let's stop at the candy store. Fifty cents. Whatever you want."

"No thanks."

"Why not?"

"I don't feel like it."

"You'll have to face John sooner or later."

My head snapped up. I knew my mother or Billy could sometimes read my thoughts but I hadn't known my father could read anything but the newspaper. "No, I won't. I'll never go in that damn store again." My first "damn" slid by, stole home.

"I think you'd better go in right now and congratulate him."

"Congratulate him! I hate him. And his damn Giants."

"If you don't go in there now, you'll never be able to. Then just seeing the candy store will be enough to make you angry all over again. Pretty soon you won't even be able to walk by it."

I didn't say anything.

"You've got to live here, Daniel."

It was the only advice my father had ever given me, the only advice he was ever to give me. For a moment I wondered if the good seats during the final game, if the entire Pennant race itself, had been engineered to this end.

I pushed open the door to the candy store. There John sat, a Buddha behind the counter.

"Congratulations," I said. "What a game," I said. "Too bad you couldn't be there." I waited with everything in my body clenched.

John's gloating smile dissolved in confusion. He was listening for the punchline. Finally, "Thanks. You were there? Hey, that's some luck. Must have really been a sight, huh?"

I nodded, put two quarters on the counter, and gathered up my consolation prize.

"Nah," he shoved the coins back, "this one's on the Giants."

As we were going out the door John called, "Hey, congratulations to you too."

I stood looking back at him, waiting for the punchline.

"Campanella. For Most Valuable Player. He deserves it."

"Thanks. See you."

"Hey, take it easy."

I counted that as the second piece of advice I'd received that day.

What happened between my parents was no more startling than my father's purchase of a car or my mother's promise to buy a television set. The world was changing and I would try to take it easy. I hoped Branca would do the same. It wasn't his fault. Thomson had already hit 31 homers that year.

About the Doris Bakwin Award

The Doris Bakwin Award for Writing by a Woman was established by Michael Bakwin in honor of his late wife, Doris Winchester Bakwin. Doris was a warm-hearted and engaged listener and storyteller. As her daughter Lisa Lindgren wrote: "My mom loved thunderstorms like most people love a beautiful sunset. She would sit by an open window and breathe it in. My earliest memory is sitting with her in a rocking chair by the screen door enjoying a storm together. I still have a strange fondness for the scent of rain on a screen. We talked of dancing in the rain. I guess that's my image of my mom – dancing in a storm – strong and happy. Her life was like that. No storm she couldn't handle." Doris always wanted to write down her own life story, but did not get to it before her death in 2004.

Carolina Wren Press gratefully acknowledges the generous contributions made by members of the Bakwin extended family. The gifts have enabled us to make the Doris Bakwin Award an on-going competition:
  ~ *Submission deadline is March 15th, in even-numbered years.*
  ~ *Full guidelines are available at www.carolinawrenpress.org.*

—Andrea Selch, President, Carolina Wren Press

The text of the book is typeset in 10-point Minion.
The book was designed by Lesley Landis Designs
and printed by BookMobile